Table of Contents

CHAPTER ONE

THE CALL

February 19, 10:00 pm

Joe

Joe Wallace had gotten home late after a very long, very rough day. He was tired, and he collapsed in front of the news. There'd been a kerfuffle in the courtroom earlier, and his client's case was going to suffer for the guy's impulsive actions. Joe had gotten smacked in the face during the melee and was probably going to be sporting a black eye tomorrow. The courtroom Marshalls nipped it in the bud quickly, but it was definitely dramatic enough to make the nightly news. His wife, Sara, brought him a beer and came and joined him on the couch. He turned the sound down on the tv while he told her about what had happened. Sara glanced at the TV and put up her hand to stop him. "Joe. Honey. What in the world? That looks like Caro's house." You could see the distinctive wreath hanging on the front door that his sister, Caroline, had made. She'd given them a matching one for Christmas. Hers was lit up by the strobe lights of the police cars surrounding the house. Joe grabbed the remote and turned up the sound.

Thomas

His phone rang just seconds before the doorbell began to chime. "It's almost 10. Who could that be?" asked Amy.

"It's Joe on the phone," he said, looking at the screen. And he answered his brother's call while she went to see who was at the door.

"Turn on your tv! THE TV! Turn it on!" Joe was screaming into his ear.

"Jo-Jo, calm down," Thomas tried to say, but Joe was sobbing now.

"Oh, God, Tommy. Oh, God, oh, God, oh God."

Thomas looked up to see Amy standing in the doorway, the color leached from her face. "Tommy," she said gently. "Something's happened. The police." Her words trailed off.

Lisa

Lisa Wallace Shepard and her husband, David, were having a date night. With five children and busy careers, they felt it was important to devote some time just to each other at least once a week. But life had been especially busy lately they'd not been out to dinner in a while. Their teenagers, Jessica and Beau, were more than capable of watching their three smaller siblings, but with tax season right around the corner this was a hard time of year for David to get away. They were in their favorite restaurant, enjoying coffee and splitting a dessert when David's phone rang. It was their daughter Jessica. Lisa's heart skipped a beat. She hoped it was something minor, but Jess was very capable and mature. She wouldn't be calling unless it was something she couldn't handle. David said, "Jess?" Even across the table, Lisa could hear her daughter's panicked voice.

Kelly

They'd let their three children stay up late watching a movie, and Stephen, God bless him, had gotten all of them bathed and put to bed. Kelly Wallace Thornton was cleaning up the kitchen. It had been a fun night, but she was tired. The doorbell rang. Stephen was still upstairs, so Kelly went to answer it. Two policemen stood on the porch.

"Mrs. Thornton?"

"Yes," said Kelly. "But I didn't call you."

"No, ma'am," said one of the officers. "Could we please come inside and talk to you and your husband?"

Thomas

Thomas could still hear Joe's screams as the phone fell out of his hand and onto the floor, and he walked into the living room.

"Dr. Wallace?" the officer asked.

"Yes," said Thomas. "Who died? You wouldn't be here at this hour for something less than that. Was it an auto accident? Please tell me. Who?"

"Let's sit down," said the officer. He told Thomas his name and his partner's name as he led him to the couch. Why on earth were they stalling? "We got a call." Thomas had already forgotten both of their names. "They wanted us to get here before you saw anything on the news."

"So, dad then." said Thomas, feeling his stomach twist. If Senator Wallace was dead it would definitely be on all the late-night news shows. And if there were people who wanted the news broken gently, it was probably some of his dad's staff. Had poor Joe seen it on the news before anyone could get to him? Dad and Mom and Michael were visiting his sister, Caroline, in Portland. He wondered who else had been in the car. He hoped no one else had died. He hoped there hadn't been pictures of twisted wreckage on the screen for Joe to see. He wondered if this scene was being played out right now at Lisa's house. And at Kelly's.

Amy's phone was ringing. Meghan's phone was ringing.

"Don't answer that, Meg!" yelled Thomas. But he heard his 15-year-old daughter's sharp intake of breath. She began to sob. Amy ran up the stairs to her, just as TJ ran down to his dad.

"Go upstairs, T. Help your mom." Thomas ordered. But 17-year-old TJ wouldn't budge. And Thomas couldn't find the energy to insist. He picked up the remote and turned on the TV.

Office Whoever said, "Sir, just give us a minute. Please."

"Tell me," begged Thomas.

And then they did. They told him as he saw his sister Caroline's house come into view on the tv screen, lit up by the flashing lights of a dozen police cars. They told him as he watched paramedics rush out of the house with someone on a stretcher. Who was it? Thomas squinted at the tv. The person on the stretcher had a bloody looking gauze wrapped around their forehead and was covered with blankets and an oxygen mask. A policeman ran alongside holding up an IV bag. His dad's bodyguard, Frank Malone, followed behind the gurney, jacket flapping in the wind. There were stains on the front of Frank's shirt. Dark curly hair couldn't be contained by the gauze. Not dad, then. It must be Caroline. Or maybe Michael? They told him as he saw reporters and camera crews race up to the police tape shouting questions. They told him as one of the cameras swung around and zoomed in very close, and he could see that it was Michael on the stretcher, and he could see blood dripping down his youngest brother's pale face. Mikey looked too still. As still as death. But would they be running if he were already dead? Thomas tried to focus. He had the absurd thought, "But this isn't a car accident." He tried to hear the words the officer was saying. A few of them got through to him. Attack. Caroline's house. Multiple victims. Death.

CHAPTER TWO

BEGINNINGS

Senator Thomas Wallace and his wife, Catherine, thought that their family was complete with four children between the ages of eight and sixteen, when the twins came along as a late-in-life surprise.

Thomas, named for his father and the eldest boy, had just finished a successful a successful sophomore year. He was the quarterback of the varsity football team, and was excited to play next year, but planned to give up sports and study medicine at Duke after graduation. If you were a Wallace, you had a plan. Or rather, the Senator had a plan for you. But Thomas was interested in medicine and happy to follow his dad's advice. Tall and athletic with wavy sand colored hair, Thomas found it easy to stay in his father's good graces. He worked hard for his excellent grades. His quick temper and passion for justice were inherited, but he had learned to control that temper most of the time. Thomas was spending that summer working at a day camp for disabled children, and after work he loved being with his family and the various friends and relatives who always seemed to be in and out of their ocean front home.

Lisa was fourteen that year. She was a pretty girl, thin and willowy with thick auburn hair and deep blue eyes. She was the editor of the school newspaper, and even at that young age knew she wanted to go to Wake Forest after graduation to study Literature and Writing. Her grades and extracurricular activities, not to mention her famous father, made it likely that she would be able to meet that goal. At first meeting, Lisa Wallace seemed quiet and retiring. She was neither. Once you got to know her, Lisa was a force to be reckoned with. She was strong in her faith and stood up for causes she believed in. Lisa had wrangled the other Wallace children, even her older brother, for years and helped keep order in the house. She often ran interference for her siblings when they came under the

Senator's scrutiny. Dad wanted them to succeed. Mom loved them. Lisa protected them.

Kelly was ten, and painfully shy. She was on the skinny side of thin and always wore her long brown hair in braids. She ducked her head in the presence of just about everyone and rarely spoke above a whisper, much to the Senator's displeasure. Kelly brought home the expected A's, though, and escaped her father's disappointment at her lack of interest in sports by being something of a musical prodigy. She gave a lackluster performance on the soccer field, because the Senator insisted that his children participate in at least one sport and play at least one musical instrument. It was the piano that saved her. She was often trotted out to play for guests, and nobody complained when she escaped to her room and buried her nose in a book as soon as possible.

Eight-year-old Joe was coming off a rather unsuccessful third grade year. Joe was an average student and clumsy at sports. His thick hair was light brown, and there was a smattering of freckles across his slightly pudgy face. Many parents would have been thrilled with a son who was hard working, kind hearted, and cheerful. But these parents were not Senator Wallace. Joe's report card, with its hard earned Bs was not at all acceptable. His seat on the bench at baseball games was embarrassing. His practice sessions on the saxophone were nerve jangling. His quiet acceptance of criticism was infuriating. But knowing that he was a disappointment hadn't darkened Jo-Jo's sunny disposition. It was hard not to love the sweet teddy bear that was Joseph Wallace. Classmates and teachers found him charming. On good days the Senator ignored him.

And then the twins were born. It had been a difficult birth, and Catherine Wallace was tired. In their early years Caroline and Michael were doted on and spoiled by everyone except their strict father. They were beautiful children with soft dark curls and deep brown eyes. It was obvious from the time they were toddlers that they were very bright. They walked early and developed extensive vocabularies before their little mouths were able to pronounce the words, which amused and delighted family and friends. Their older siblings called them Caro and Mikey. But in trying to call his sister "sissy" Michael called her C. And in trying to call him "brother" she called him Bubba. The nicknames stuck. If they ran a bit wild as toddlers, it was because Catherine was too exhausted to rein them in, and their siblings were too charmed by them to ever say no. Still, there was a strong competitive streak and will to succeed running deep in the Wallace blood, and by the time the twins were in school they had taken the difficult mantle of making Senator Wallace proud upon their young shoulders.

Caroline, feisty, strong willed, and whip smart had taken command of their hearts immediately. She was fiercely loyal, especially to her less outgoing twin. Caroline did enthusiastic battle with those she loved, and was a fearful force to the few she didn't. Her long brown curls could be seen blowing in the wind as she sprinted across the finish line of a race, or just as often, as she knocked down a child twice her size who dared to do something that went against her rather lengthy and strict code of honor. Being unkind to her brother, Michael, was at the top of that list, and no one ever tried that more than once if Caroline Wallace was nearby.

Michael was the baby, just minutes younger than his sister, but it soon became apparent to everyone that he was the crown prince of the family. He was brilliant, athletic, and charismatic, but also kind hearted and quiet. There didn't seem to be anything Mikey wasn't good at. He made schoolwork and athletic games look effortless. He played the piano beautifully. And Michael, even as a small child, would pick less popular children to be on the team that he had invariably been chosen to captain. Teammates soon learned not to complain about Michael's choices. If they weren't afraid of his displeasure, they certainly didn't want to deal with Caroline's fiery wrath. Mikey befriended lonely children, inviting them to sit with him at lunch, or be in his study group, or even come out to his family's home at the weekend to play, swim in the pool, and picnic on the beach. He never made them feel that it was a favor, and indeed it wasn't. He would have been genuinely surprised to find out that anyone thought these things were out of the ordinary, and was totally oblivious to the power of his charm and personality. There was something very special about Mikey Wallace. Everyone adored him.

CHAPTER THREE

MICHAEL

February 19, 4:00 pm

Michael tried slipping quietly out of his sister's house on the pretext of getting the feel of the church and making sure things were set up properly, but Caroline always saw right through him.

"You just don't want to eat before you give your talk," Caro accused. "Did you even have breakfast or lunch?"

"Shh! For crying out loud don't let Mom hear you." he pleaded. Caroline smirked.

"Mom! Michael is leaving and he hasn't had anything to eat all day."

Michael straightened his back and stared at his twin. "Mom. Caroline has been sneaking cigarettes out in the back yard."

Catherine Wallace walked into the room and sighed. "As if I haven't been hearing this bickering for the last 30 years." She kissed Michael's cheek and pushed a granola bar into his hand. "You! Eat something." She commanded. "And as for you, missy..."

As Michael made his escape, he heard Caro saying, "Honestly, Mom. Why the hell do you always let him get away with everything?"

"Language, Caroline Mary!" said Catherine.

"Sorry, Mom. I mean it, though. He is so spoiled."

Michael smiled. It was good to be with his parents and his sister and brother-in-law and their brood for a few days, even if Caro had roped him into speaking at a Mission at her church. For all their arguing, Michael adored Caro, and she him. They would do anything for each other.

****

Frank Malone had been one of his dad's bodyguards for as long as Michael could remember. He was a former FBI agent who had started his own security company. Tonight, the Senator asked Frank to make sure his son got to the church and home again safely. Frank's partner, Gerry Pelton, would stay behind with the rest of the family. Michael was embarrassed to have a driver. He was a grown man, and could get himself where he needed to be, thank you very much. But Senator Wallace had been receiving more than the usual number of odd letters and death threats and was not about to have his son driving around an unfamiliar city alone. And one just did not say no to Senator Wallace. Particularly when one was his son. For his part, Frank was glad to spend some time with the youngest Wallace child. He'd gotten to know the family very well in the years he'd worked for the Senator, and Michael was secretly his favorite of the six siblings. Technically both Michael and Caroline were the youngest, but Caro had always had a streak of tough independence that made her seem older than her quiet sensitive twin.

"You don't have to wait here with me, Frank," said Michael as they pulled up to the church. "There are hours before the Mission starts. I'm fine."

"I'll just find a place to park the car and sit in the back," Frank answered. "I won't bother you."

Michael colored. "You don't bother me, Frank. It's just that I hate to take you away from your job." The truth was that he didn't want to feel that he had a babysitter, and they both knew it.

"Well apparently you're my assignment tonight, Michael, so I'll just hang around." Frank knew it had always irked Michael when his family treated him like a child. But Frank, like everyone else, would never for a minute consider neglecting the Senator's orders. If driving Michael around and keeping him safe was the task he was given, then he was certainly going to do just that.

The church was unlocked. It was silent and still when Michael walked in, and he assumed he was alone. The Mission wasn't scheduled to start until 7:00. He had lied to Caroline about wanting to make sure things were ready for his talk. The local people would take care of that. Michael needed time to unwind and try to beat back his anxiety. He was tired, having been up most of the previous night working on his talks. He'd flown in from North Carolina just this morning, and his usual pre-talk jitters had already kicked in. There was a piano at the front near the altar. Since he was alone, Michael walked to it, sat down, and began to play. Nothing had ever calmed him like playing the piano. The church was freezing, so he didn't remove his overcoat or the plaid scarf which was wrapped around his neck.

"Young man! What do you think you're doing?"

Michael, startled, flinched and hit the wrong keys which sounded a jarring chord. A stern-faced woman was standing behind him looking down over the top of her glasses. He'd been so immersed in the music that he hadn't heard her come in.

"Oh, I'm sorry. I thought it would be alright." Michael stammered.

"You can't just waltz into a church and start playing the piano!" The woman sounded more exasperated than angry. "We're having a Mission here tonight, or the doors wouldn't even be unlocked. "

"Oh. Yes. I'm. Um. I'm Michael Wallace," he answered, wondering for a split second if he was in the right church.

"You're *Father* Wallace?" she asked with a decided air of skepticism. Michael cursed his youthful looks for the millionth time. He unwound his scarf and slipped out of his coat so she could see his clerical collar.

"Yes. I'm very sorry. I suppose I should have checked in with someone. With you. But the church seemed empty and I didn't think anyone would mind," he gestured vaguely at the piano.

The woman laughed. "I'm the one who's sorry, Father Wallace. If I'd seen your face, I would have recognized you. Your picture is on the brochure, and you look very like your sister. You just caught me off guard. I didn't expect you until later. I'm Margaret Porter, the Parish Administrator. Father Kendal is in a meeting, but will be over at 6:30. Please feel free to play the piano as long as you want. Can I get you anything? Do you have dinner plans?"

"Actually," said Michael, "I'd like to find a quiet room where I can be out of the way to prepare and pray before we begin, if that's possible. And thank you, but I'll have dinner later at home with my family."

Michael always asked for a private room at speaking engagements. He told them it was to prepare and pray, which was partially true. When he was lucky it had an attached, or at least a nearby bathroom. He had learned to keep his stomach empty on the days he spoke, so he hadn't thrown up before a talk in some time. It was always a possibility, though, and he felt more queasy than usual today. Knowing that his dad would be in the front pew did not help his jangled nerves at all.

****

Michael could hold a crowd in the palm of his hand. Tonight, the church was packed, but as usual he looked relaxed and natural to everyone in the pews. Being an eloquent speaker, smart, charismatic, and charming, was his blessing, but it was also his curse. It wasn't the speaking, really, that amped up his anxiety. Giving homilies to his home parish was a joy. It was the huge crowds of strangers that always unsettled him. Nobody but Caro knew how much it cost him to do this, and she felt a bit guilty about agreeing when her pastor suggested that her brother would be an excellent choice for their mission. "After all," she reasoned, "If it wasn't here, Mikey would probably be speaking someplace else." She knew it was selfish, but she wanted to show her clever brother off to her fellow parishioners.

Michael never said no when asked to give these talks. Only once had he casually mentioned his anxiety to the Senator. He told his father he was considering asking the Bishop to stop assigning him to give talks. He enjoyed writing. He would happily write the talks if only some else would give them. The senator looked at him and laughed. "Do you think all those people are packing the pews for your words? Don't be naïve, Michael. Three fourths of them are coming for those curls and dimples." Michael reddened with hurt and anger. The unkind statement wounded, but did not surprise him. Nobody could hurt him like the Senator, and yet he strove every day to please him. His dad, seeing he had gone too far, added, "I'm not saying that once they get there your words don't impact them, Michael. I'm just saying that God gave you more than one gift. He made you a good public speaker. It would be slapping Him in the face to throw it away." So Michael continued to deal with his anxiety and unsettled stomach.

It had really touched a nerve, though, when his dad implied his looks were bringing people to his talks. So shortly after the encounter he told his brother, Joe, "I'm thinking about shaving my head."

Catherine Wallace walked into the room. "What on earth? Why would you do that?"

"I don't know, Mom. This mop is kind of a pain. And it might be cooler in the summer."

Catherine took his face in her hands. "You'll shave your head over my dead body, Michael Joseph. And even then I'll come back from the grave and haunt you. I did not spend years of my life untangling that hair for you to cut it all off."

****

Tonight, Michael spoke about forgiveness. He started with God's forgiveness and the beauty of the Sacrament of Reconciliation. Then he spoke about the importance of forgiving each other. And he ended by speaking about the importance of forgiving ourselves.

"Some of you may know my sister, Caroline."

Caro, in the front row with her husband, Matt, their two oldest children, Matt's parents, and Senator and Mrs. Wallace looked up sharply. "What are you doing, *Father*?" she said audibly.

Michael smiled. "Hi, Caro." He winked at her.

"I want to tell you a story about Caroline and me. When we were eight years old, my sister pushed me down the very steep front steps of our home, and I broke my arm." Caro shook her head and glared at him. Michael grinned sheepishly.

"Sorry, C. To be fair to my sister, I very much deserved the push, although probably not the broken arm. You see, we were fiercely competitive. And we were lucky. It wasn't terribly good for our egos, but we usually won at whatever we tried. Sometimes I came in first and Caro came in second. Sometimes it was the reverse. Running races, math competitions, and spelling bees really brought out our sibling rivalry. Looking back, I think it was good for me to lose once in a while, because when I finally grew old enough to reflect, I was able to work on, and hopefully develop, some sorely needed humility. But at eight years old coming in second to my sister made me jealous and angry.

There was a competition at school that day. I can't even remember what it was. Do you remember, Caro?"

She shook her head and looked down, memories flooding in.

"Whatever it was, Caroline won. And I was angry. When we got home from school, I went straight into her room and ripped the head off her new Build a Bear." He laughed. "I guess you could say I had a bit of a temper. Caro came in and saw what I'd done and went absolutely berserk. She started chasing me through the house and screaming. To be honest, this was kind of the usual state of affairs at our house, and I can't imagine how our poor mother put up with it. I'm pretty sure she's a saint." He smiled at Catherine.

"Anyway, I ran out onto the porch. As Caroline caught up with me, she reached out and gave a push. I know she didn't realize how close we were to the stairs.

Now I was the type of child to who liked make a big fuss about things, and a broken arm would usually have been a great opportunity for some extra attention. And it hurt a lot. But I looked up and saw my sister's eyes filling with the horror of what she'd done, and I think I grew up a little bit that day. I forgave her immediately. I told her that it wasn't her fault, that I had tripped. I tried to tell mom that I had just tripped and fallen, but Caro's guilt made her confess to the push. Everyone knew she never meant to hurt me, but she was devastated. My brothers and sisters and mom and dad all told her they knew she didn't want to hurt me. They told her they forgave her. I told her that I forgave her. Mom took her to confession and God certainly forgave her. But she could not forgive herself."

Michael looked over to see tears in Caroline's eyes and, in fact, in the eyes of some of the parishioners. "For as long as I had that cast on, Caroline waited on me hand and foot. She couldn't do enough for me. She purposely missed a word in the next spelling bee so that I could win. Which was a hollow victory, by the way, Caro. I was perfectly aware that you knew how to spell neighbor."

Everyone laughed.

"For weeks Caroline's guilt ate at her. She could not forgive herself for causing me to be hurt. Her school work suffered. She couldn't concentrate. She couldn't sleep.

Things got better when the doctor removed my cast, and we went back to our normal life of crazy sibling rivalry mixed with a lot of love. But do you want to know something? Even after all these years, I don't think my sister has forgiven herself for that one rash act. And I want to tell her something tonight. And I want to tell all of you something. God loves you. His love is real. After you repent and confess, it's time to forgive yourself."

"It's ok, C," he whispered.

Senator Wallace shook Michael's hand. "I'm proud of you, son." Michael looked at him in surprise. The Senator had been bitterly disappointed when his brilliant youngest son stood up to him for the very first time and entered the seminary. He'd spent most of the time since finding fault with everything Michael did. It was not the life he had mapped out for the son whom he had always thought was the one with the most potential. And even in the best of times the Senator's compliments had been few and far between.

Catherine hugged him. "When do you think you'll be back at the house?"

Michael looked at his watch. "Well, I really need to stay at the reception for a couple of hours. People usually want to talk. It will probably be at least 10:30 or 11:00."

Matt shook his hand and said, "Good talk, Mikey. I'd not heard that broken arm story before."

And then Caroline was hugging him. "I love you, Bubba, you big goofball. I'll fix you something to eat when you get home."

Michael whispered, "Thanks, C. Love you, too. I don't know if I'm more tired or hungry. See you soon."

It was only about 15 minutes later that the power went out. There wasn't a storm. People speculated that a car had hit a nearby transformer. The reception hall was eerily dark and getting very cold on this chilly night. Father Kendal announced that they would have to leave, but that Father Wallace would be returning to give another talk the next night. He also said that Father Wallace had volunteered to be available during the day for anyone who might want to talk to him. Frank, who was paid to notice things, knew how Michael felt about people crowding around him. He decided to rescue Michael, and appeared with his coat and scarf saying that they'd better get going.

Margaret Porter walked up to Michael. "I heard you telling your sister that you were hungry, Father, so I grabbed a couple of cookies from the buffet table to tide you over. Consider it a peace offering after the piano misunderstanding. They're lemon."

Michael laughed. "No peace offering needed, but thank you. The misunderstanding was totally my fault. How did you know lemon was my favorite?"

Margaret smiled at him. "The whole parish knows that lemon is your favorite. Caroline told us, and there's a long table full of lemon desserts in the gathering room. We'll save them for tomorrow night."

****

"Looks like I'll get you home shortly after 9:00, Mikey," said Frank as they drove along the dark streets. "It'll be nice surprise for your folks to have an extra couple of hours to visit with you."

"Feels like 1:00 in the morning to me, Frank. I am dead on my feet." Michael answered, munching on a lemon cookie. "Want one? They're really good."

"No, thanks. You're the one who hasn't eaten all day." When they arrived at the house he added, "It doesn't look like there are any parking places on the street, and the driveway is full of cars. I may have to double-park for a bit."

Michael looked at him. "Are you serious? You do not have to walk me in. The house is literally right there, Frank. What could happen to me?"

Frank knew he should probably go in the house and check in with the Senator. But he also didn't want Michael to feel he was being treated like a child yet again. He laughed. "Ok. I'm beat, too, if I'm being honest. I'll drop you here and go to the hotel. Tell your dad I'll be here at 8:00 tomorrow morning to take over from Gerry."

The house was dark. Michael was surprised that they hadn't left the porch light on for him, but it looked like there was a dim light in the kitchen so he made his way down the driveway to the back door. Frank watched from the car until he saw Michael open the door and step into the mudroom, then drove away grateful that he was finally going to be able to get some sleep. The mudroom door hadn't been locked, and as Michael entered, he tripped over a pair of carelessly discarded cowboy boots. He picked them up and set them neatly aside. Then he turned the handle on the kitchen door and opened it.

CHAPTER FOUR

THE SENATOR

Senator Thomas Wallace loved his family with all his heart. But his love was a smothering, exacting, demanding thing. He was a hard man to please. He showered his children with attention when he could and with all the time he had to give. He went to their school events, sporting events, and recitals. He swam with them, played games with them, and read to them. He took them on vacations and bought them expensive gifts. And he had absolutely no understanding of the way his impossible expectations affected them. His children were drowning in the rough seas of trying to please him. All of them developed coping skills, some better than others. Thomas was quick to anger, but was able to work his aggressions out on the football field. Lisa had an extreme need to please, Joe lacked motivation, and Kelly barely spoke. Caroline shared Thomas's temper and fought the world. And Michael? Well, Michael simply internalized everything.

The Senator was usually gone during the week, but he made it a point to be home on Friday afternoons and through the weekend as often as he could. On Fridays before dinner, you handed your weekly school reports and papers to Dad. Tommy and Lisa were off at college, but the four younger Wallace children dutifully lined up at their father's desk each week.

On this Friday the Senator glanced at Kelly's perfect report, signed it, and handed it back without a word. Kelly was the invisible child. She did what was expected and then faded silently into the background. Dad frowned at Joe's papers, muttered, "For God's sake. If you'd only try. Are you a Wallace or not?" and then gave it up and signed the packet in disgust. They'd had this conversation too many times before. Joe hung his head and stepped back. You remained in the room to hear what Dad had to say to everyone. This was a rule. If you got the extremely rare word of praise your siblings would hear it, and presumably be inspired. If you got berated, they would hear that as well, and hopefully shape up.

Finally, the Senator turned to his favorites. Being one of the Senator's favorites came with a price. You simply had to be perfect in everything you did. Caroline skipped forward and shoved her dark curls behind her ears. Senator Wallace smiled at her report, signed it with a flourish, and patted her on the head. Eight-year-old Michael stepped forward solemnly. The Senator beamed at his brightest star, but then his smile faded. Michael's packet of papers held a math test. There was a large B written on the top in red ink. The senator looked down at him and said, "You've disappointed me, son." He signed the packet and threw it on the table, not bothering to hand it back.

Senator Wallace did not speak to his youngest son at dinner that night. He did not go into Michael's room to say good-night at bedtime. The following day he did not appear at the baseball game where Michael did an excellent job of pitching and hit a home run. He did not shake Michael's hand in church during the Sign of Peace. When his dad went back to Washington DC for the week, Michael was not invited to tell the Senator about his day, or even appear on the nightly FaceTime calls. The Senator did not speak a word to the boy, or give him a glance, for the entire week. Late Thursday night Joe heard his brother sobbing and went in and sat on his bed. "It's ok, Mikey. It's just one B. I mean, I'm the dumb one. You're a genius or something, and he's wrong to make you feel so bad."

Michael sat up and hugged him. "You're not dumb, Jo-Jo. You're one of the smartest people I know, because you know how to make people feel better when they're sad. That's really important. I think dad just doesn't understand that there are lots of ways to be smart. I know I didn't study enough for the math test. I'll try harder next time. He just wants us to do our best.

The following Friday, the Wallace children lined up as usual and handed the Senator their papers. When Michael handed him the packet of perfect papers, his dad flipped through them, signed the pack, handed it back, and said the first words he had spoken to his son in a week, "What time is your game tomorrow, son?" Michael Wallace never again got a grade lower than an A.

CHAPTER FIVE

LISA

February 20, 1:00 am

The police said that it might be a good idea for them to all be in one place so they'd be easier to protect. Lisa could not wrap her head around needing to be protected. Her dad had always been a moderate with conservative leanings, but lately the political atmosphere had become charged and he'd been attacked by both right- and left-wing fanatics. It seemed like dad couldn't please anybody anymore. He tried to address concerns in a logical calm way, but had been receiving the nastiest letters and even death threats. He said they were mostly from crackpots and laughed them off to his children, but they still worried. And now it looked as though their fears had come true.

So they all gathered at Lisa's beautiful ocean front home. They always did that, even though mom and dad had a house just four down from Lisa and David. The beach sand probably held hundreds or thousands of the footsteps of Wallace children and grandchildren running back and forth between the two. Lisa's house was large and comfortable and usually full of laughing kids. The Wallaces tended to have what was considered, in these days, large families. Lisa and David had five children. Tommy and Amy, and Joe and Sarah had four. Kelly and Stephen had three. And Caroline and Matt, well, they had had four children. Two of them were still alive, but try as she might Lisa could not find out the condition of any of the survivors of the brutal attack. Her brother Mikey was the only one she'd seen briefly on the TV screen, and every few minutes one of her siblings would obsessively rewind and watch again and speculate on his condition. Tommy was on a hastily chartered jet heading toward Portland and would call them with information as soon as he could.

Lisa had gotten him the flight. She was a planner. She took pride in being organized. Tommy was older by two years, but as the eldest daughter, Lisa was used to being a helper. She had taken care of the twins when they were babies and loved them as if they were her own children instead of her brother and sister. All of her siblings had always turned to her for advice. If you had a problem, Lisa was the one who would help you to solve it. Mom and dad were just too busy, and Lisa was happy to step in. But now she was at a loss. She wanted to be in Portland with Tommy and Michael and Matt and those poor hurt children. They all did. But it would take organizing - people to watch the children, flights, luggage, someplace to stay. These were the things she was good at. But Lisa felt paralyzed. She just couldn't think. Beyond getting Tommy's flight scheduled she couldn't even pick up the phone, let alone formulate a plan. She felt paralyzed with grief.

And so she stayed in the family room of this lovely home, sitting with her remaining siblings. Some of the littlest children had fallen asleep upstairs. The teenagers were huddled in weepy masses in the basement recreation room. The seven adults were almost silent, crushed by their grief and terrified to think of what they still had to lose. Their brother, Michael, their brother-in-law, Matt, 6-year-old Anne, and 4-year-old Paul were still alive as far as they knew. Their mom had survived briefly, but they had just been informed that she died on the way to the hospital. It was another devastating blow, and they were reeling from the news. The cable channels were not listing the names of those who had died until the all of the family was notified, but broadcasters speculated that Senator Wallace was one of the murder victims. Aunts and uncles, cousins and friends needed to be called, but the Wallace children couldn't bear to make those calls just yet. They knew exactly who they had lost, and the names kept throbbing in their aching heads. Dad. Mom. Caroline. The kids, 7-year-old Greg and tiny Madison, just 3 years old. And one of dad's bodyguards, Gerry Pelton.

CHAPTER SIX

ULCER

"I throwed up."

Senator Wallace turned the page of the newspaper he was reading without looking up. "Threw is the past tense of throw, Michael. You threw up."

"It was red," Michael said, barely above a whisper. His voice trembled.

Lisa looked up from the paper she was writing. "Dad!" she said, sharply. "He's bleeding."

There were tests in the emergency room and scopes after he was admitted to the hospital, and then they got surprising news. Why in the world would this bright, sunny, uncomplaining nine-year-old have an ulcer? It was so hard to understand. He didn't have any food allergies. Every test seemed to come back with normal results.

Twenty-six-year-old Thomas, who was doing a psych rotation in medical school, knew a wonderful psychiatrist, and they reluctantly made an appointment. After all, this child had everything. His parents and siblings loved him. He was good at schoolwork, sports, and music. Children at school wanted to be his friend. Surely he didn't need a psychiatrist.

"Michael, they tell me you're a pretty smart guy, so I'm not going to beat around the bush. I'm going to ask you some questions, and I hope you'll tell me the truth. Ok?"

"Yes, sir. I will."

"Michael, is something making you unhappy?"

"No, sir."

"Are you afraid of something? Anxious about something?"

"No, sir."

"Would you tell me if you were?"

Michael thought a minute. "Yes, sir. I would. I promised my dad I'd think carefully about all the questions and answer them."

"Michael, you don't have to call me sir."

"Ok. Thank you, sir."

"How are things going at school?"

"Fine. I like school. I just wish…"

"What do you wish, Michael?"

"I wish it was easy for Jo-Jo, too. He has to work really hard."

"Are you worried about your brother, Joe?"

"Not really. I just sometimes wish he didn't have to work so hard."

"What are your favorite things to do, Michael?"

Michael relaxed visibly. "I like to play the piano. That's the best. Oh, and I like to read, and play baseball, and swim. And I like to have picnics on the beach with the whole family and have a bonfire and make s'mores."

"Michael, do you know what a perfectionist is?"

"No, sir."

"Well, it's a person who feels it's very important for everything to be perfect. They tell me that you always get A's at school."

"I got a B once," Michael said softly.

"But that's ok. You know that's ok, right?"

Michael shook his head sadly. "It's not my best."

The doctor said, "Well, they also tell me that you change your shirt a lot if even the smallest thing gets spilled on it. And when you roast a marshmallow, it is always perfectly browned. They say you start a piano piece over if you make a mistake instead of muddling on. Things like that."

"Are those things bad, sir?"

"Oh, no. They're not bad. Unless it makes you upset when things aren't perfect. Then it could be a problem. Does it upset you to have a burned marshmallow or a shirt with a stain on it?"

Michael thought a moment. "I don't know. I like the brown marshmallows, not the burned ones. And I like clean shirts. I don't know."

"What about friends? Do you have friends besides your brothers and sisters?"

Michael nodded. "Yes. Lots of them. Sometimes I get to invite them over to swim, or I get to go to their houses to play."

"Are any of your friends mad at you?"

"I don't think so." Michael wrinkled his forehead and asked, "Sir? Could you please tell me what I did wrong?

"Why do you think you did something wrong, Michael?"

"Well, Jo-jo said I was going to a head shrinker. I guess that means I did something wrong. Only I can't figure out what I did. Was it too many clean shirts?"

"Michael, seeing a psychiatrist doesn't mean you did anything wrong. Lots of people come and talk to me when they have a problem they want to figure out."

"But I don't have a problem I want to figure out."

"What about your stomach aches? Do you want to figure them out?"

"Sure. But aren't they because I have the flu or something?"

"That's one of the things we're trying to figure out. You don't seem to have the flu. Sometimes people get stomach aches when they are anxious or upset. We're just trying to find out if anything is bothering you. Ok?"

"Ok. But nothing is bothering me."

"I can see that. But can you just answer a few more questions? Michael, do you love your dad and mom?"

"Of course. Yes, sir."

"Well, I've heard that your dad can be pretty strict. Is that true?"

Michael screwed up his face, "I don't know. I guess he wants us to do our best."

"Does he ever hit you?

Michael laughed. "No. Well, he hit me with a basketball once, but we were just playing a game and I got in the way. Do you mean like that?"

"Um. No." The psychiatrist stifled a smile. "You just turned nine, right?"

"Yes, sir."

"Do you ever wish you didn't have to share your birthday with your sister?"

"Why would I wish that? It's Caro's birthday, too. We get our own presents and stuff. We always have a big party. If the weather is nice, we have it down on the beach. It's so much fun! My mom always makes Caro a chocolate cake 'cause that's her favorite, and she always makes a lemon cake for me, 'cause that's my favorite. We get to have a piece of each other's cakes, too, so we get two pieces of cake. Nobody else gets two pieces of cake. Just Caro and me." He hesitated. "Sir? Will I have to stop eating lemon cake because of the stomach aches?"

The psychiatrist reported that while he had some minor anxiety Michael seemed to be a well-adjusted, happy, chatty child. He was also a child with a bleeding ulcer, and Michael's stomach continued to rebel against him throughout his life.

CHAPTER SEVEN

CAROLINE'S HOUSE

February 19, 9:15 pm

Michael

The kitchen was only dimly lit. The minute he stepped through the door, Michael was confused. Something was dripping down the front of the refrigerator. Both Caroline and Matt were fussily tidy housekeepers. Where was everybody? Why had they not cleaned this up? And hadn't Caro said she was making his favorite chicken and noodles dish? This looked to be... spaghetti sauce?

Michael took another step into the kitchen. The sauce wasn't just on the refrigerator door. It was everywhere.

****

Frank

His head had barely hit the pillow when his phone rang.
"Frank Malone."

"Mr. Malone? This is Sergeant Andy Logan with the Portland police. Our local FBI office asked us to call you. I understand you're with Senator Wallace's security detail. There's been a disturbance at the house of his daughter, Caroline Carter."

A jolt of adrenaline shot through Frank. "What kind of disturbance?"

"Apparently a 4-year-old boy pounded on a neighbor's door and said that bad men were hurting his mommy. The boy looked to be injured and was wild with terror."

Frank was grabbing his clothes. "My partner, Gerry Pelton, is at the house."

"He's not answering his phone, sir."

Frank had never driven so fast in his life. He screamed up to the house and slammed on the brakes, leaving his car in the middle of the street. There were a dozen police cars and two ambulances blocking his way. He ran up to the policeman guarding the front door, flashed his credentials, and said, "Frank Malone. I'm in charge of Senator Wallace's security detail."

"Yeah? Good job," said the young cop.

Frank didn't even bother to be annoyed. The guy looked decidedly green around the gills, which told Frank all he needed to know about what could be found inside of that house. He brushed by and walked through the front door. An FBI agent from the local office stopped him and he explained once again who he was.

"What's the situation?" Frank asked, trying to keep his nerves in check.

"One man, one woman, and two children have been transported to the hospital with a variety of wounds. The others in the house are all deceased. It would be helpful if you could formally identify them."

"Was the man who was taken to the hospital Senator Wallace?"

"No. It was Matthew Carter, the senator's son-in-law. Also taken were Mrs. Catherine Wallace, a young girl and the boy who alerted the neighbor."

"How serious were their injuries," Frank asked.

"The little boy looked to have a broken arm and bad bump on the head. Possible concussion. Mr. Carter was semi-conscious and incoherent. Mrs. Wallace and the girl were unconscious. All three were drenched in blood. I didn't see the full extent of their injuries."

"I had a partner working here tonight. Gerry Pelton."

"I'm sorry. He's in the backyard. They got him before they ever entered the house."

Frank struggled to control his emotions and shook his head sadly. "Gerry was a good man. The best." He continued, "I can make the IDs. I've worked with the family for years."

"Watch where you step. Forensics is working."

Frank put paper booties over his shoes, pulled on some vinyl gloves and walked carefully into the house. The dining room was to the right, and he looked in. There was a lot of blood splashed on the table and walls, but no bodies. The family room was on the left side of the hall. Senator Wallace lay sprawled on the floor in a pool of blood, obviously dead. There was a huge gash across his throat. Caroline Carter was across the room. She had what looked like multiple stab wounds, and her throat had also been cut. Michael Wallace lay on the floor near his twin, their dark curls almost touching. His right leg was bent at the knee at an impossible angle. He still wore his overcoat. It was flung open and a dark stain had soaked through his shirt. More dark stains covered his coat sleeves, and his hands looked like they had been dipped in red paint. Defensive injuries, Frank thought idly. Blood trickled slowly from Michael's forehead and from a nasty wound on his cheek.

Frank crouched down next to him, and his voice broke as he spoke. "Oh, Mikey. I am so very sorry."

Michael's eyelids fluttered.

CHAPTER EIGHT

BIRTHDAY

When the twins turned 27 there was a large party as usual. Family, friends, and neighbors all gathered at Lisa and David's spacious house. The party spilled out onto the patio surrounding the pool and down onto the beach.

Michael, newly ordained, was a little late due to officiating at a wedding that afternoon.

"Hey, it's the birthday boy," said Thomas when he walked in. He slung his arm around his brother's neck and handed him a beer. You look pretty damn official in those priest clothes."

"Language, Thomas Gabriel," said Catherine.

"Sorry, Mom."

"And in front of a priest," said Michael shaking his head. "Shocking." He grinned and went to kiss his mother.

Karaoke music was playing and the siblings started to chant, "Mi-key. Mi-key. Mi-key." Michael had a wonderful voice and they loved to be his backup singers. Michael jumped into their midst, beer in one hand and a microphone in the other and began a rendition of "For the Longest Time" that Billy Joel would have been proud of. His brothers and brothers-in-law backed him up. During the last verse he put down the beer and microphone, pulled his mother out of her chair and danced with her to much cheering and laughter. Then the music ended.

"Michael." It was Senator Wallace speaking quietly. "Go over to the house and change."

Michael looked at his father in surprise. "Ok, dad. But why?"

The senator glanced at the friends and neighbors milling around. "It's not seemly for you to be drinking beer and singing questionable songs with those clerical clothes on."

Michael was flabbergasted. "Dad. There's nothing wrong with having one beer. And that song...."

The senator glared at his son. Michael walked down the beach to his parents' home and changed into shorts and a sweatshirt.

"Come on, dad," said Lisa. "He's just having a good time. It's his birthday."

Senator Wallace looked around at the party guests again. "It's for his own good. It doesn't look right," he said. "And let that be the end of it."

Later after most of the non-family guests had left, the senator asked Michael to play the piano. "Play something for your mother."

Michael, whose good mood had been restored by a rather large piece of lemon cake, looked at his mother innocently. "Hmmm. I don't know which song she likes." Catherine threw a pillow at him as he began to play her favorite, Chopin Nocturne Op.9. She smiled and leaned her head on her husband's shoulder.

"That's a baby song, Mikey," Caro whispered. "Annie could probably play that one." He stuck out his tongue and continued.

Afterwards he played his father's favorite song. The senator always requested "Heroic" Polonaise, op. 53, also by Chopin, but much more technically difficult. He always enjoyed seeing their friends marvel at his handsome son and the way Michael's fingers flew effortlessly over the keys. Finally, it was Caro's chance for a request.

"You know what I want, Bubba. And I want you to play the entire song. Today is the day. It will be your birthday present to me." It was their usual schtick. Michael always played exactly half of her favorite song and then switched to something silly in the middle. Then she would ask him when he would play the whole song, and he would promise her that he would definitely play the whole thing for her someday, but this wasn't the day. Michael grinned at her and began to softly play Rachmaninoff's Rhapsody on a Theme of Paganini. He didn't care for the schmaltzy song himself, but played it soulfully halfway through. Then, with mischief in his eyes, he switched to "Sweet Caroline" and loudly sang along. Caro shrieked and raced toward him, a spatula held high over her head. Michael jumped up from the piano and grabbed her in a bear hug. Somehow in the mad struggle Caro's knee came up.

"Ahhhh," said Michael dropping her and bending over. "Caro kicked me in the balls."

"Language, Michael Joseph!" exclaimed his mom.

Michael was laughing and crying at the same time. "That's not bad language, Mom. It's just bad taste."

Caroline looked stricken. "Oh, Bubba. I didn't mean to. Really I didn't."

His young niece, Rosie, came running into the room and said, "Come and swim with us, Uncle Mikey. We're going to play Chicken. I want to sit on your shoulders."

"Give me a minute, honey," groaned Michael. "Your aunt Caro kicked me in the… um… leg."

"The leg?" asked Rosie innocently. "I thought she kicked you in the balls."

"Michael Joseph Wallace!" sputtered his mom, as the whole room erupted into laughter. "Look what you've done now. Corrupting these babies!"

Michael was chastened. "I'm truly sorry, Mom," he said. "It won't happen again."

The younger children ran outside to the pool.

"Well," said Catherine. "I forgive you this time. But the next time you want to discuss your balls, please talk to your father." Michael collapsed on the sofa in a puddle of laughter.

The Wallace children laughed about this exchange between Mikey and their very proper mother every time they got together from that day forward.

CHAPTER NINE

HOSPITAL

February 20, 6:00 am

Thomas

When the plane landed, a car was waiting to take Thomas to the hospital. Lisa had seen to that. He wanted to scream at the driver to go faster, but instead kept repeating frantic prayers. He'd talked to Lisa the minute his plane landed and gotten the crushing news that his mom had died in the ambulance on the way to the hospital and they'd lost little Anne on the operating table as they desperately tried to save her. Matt and Paul had some serious injuries, but were going to be ok. Michael was the only survivor who was in danger now. They couldn't lose him. They just couldn't. He jumped out of the car and ran into the hospital where there were several policemen inside the lobby.

Thomas rushed up to the desk and said, "I'm Dr. Thomas Wallace. I'm looking for my brother, Michael." That caught the attention of the policemen who began walking over to him. "Dr. Wallace. We'd like to talk to you."

"Not now! I have to see my brother."

The receptionist spoke up. "I've been told that your brother has just come out of surgery and is in the recovery room. I can direct you to a waiting room, and Dr. Manton will contact you there."

Thomas turned to her. Exhaustion, grief, and a pounding headache were making him angry and on the edge of hysteria.

He spoke through gritted teeth. "Listen to me. I lost a huge part of my family last night. I am not going to a waiting room. I need to see my brother. And I will see him. Now!"

A man in scrubs walked over and put his hand gently on Thomas' arm. "Dr. Wallace? I'm Dr. Fred Manton. I've been taking care of your brother. Let's go upstairs. I'll take you to see him and we can talk along the way."

"So, Michael is alive?"

"Michael is alive."

Thomas almost collapsed with relief.

****

"Tommy? May I come in?" Frank Malone waited at the door, not wanting to intrude. He had been up all night, talking to the local FBI agents and police. He hadn't been back to the hotel to change, so he kept his jacket on and zipped in the warm room. Frank did not want Tommy to see Michael's blood smeared all over his shirt.

Thomas was sitting in a chair next to his brother's bed staring at Michael, watching his every breath. The room was dimly lit and quiet, except for the beeping of monitors. There was a towel draped across Michael's midsection. His right leg was propped on a pillow, the knee heavily bandaged. Pneumatic pressure devices on his legs hissed softly as they filled with air and then relaxed, keeping his blood flowing to prevent clots. Pillows supported his bandaged hands and arms, and there were braces on both arms. A large gauze bandage was wrapped around his lower chest with a drainage tube poking out. He had a chest tube on his left side and another on his right. There were IVs in both of his arms and wires stuck to his chest with small squares. A gauze bandage was taped over his right shoulder. Another bandage circled his head and there was a nasty looking wound on his right cheek where it had been hastily stitched closed. A ventilator tube forced air into his lungs. He was very pale and still.

"He's going to have a scar on his face," murmured Frank. "He'll like that."

"Look at him, Frank," said Thomas, as if he hadn't heard. "Look at our sweet boy. I've been a doctor for 20 years, and I've never seen someone injured this badly survive. How am I going to tell the others? We can't lose him, Frank. We will not be able to bear another loss. It will end us. We just can't." He glanced at his brother and blanched. He reached over and rubbed Michael's left shoulder, one of the few spots on his body that wasn't injured. "Oh, Mikey, I'm so sorry. You have to forgive me. My brain is wrecked with all that's happened. Of course I believe you can get well. You will get well! We need you, Bubba. Please don't leave us. Please keep fighting. I believe in you." Michael did not respond. His only movement was the rise and fall of his chest as the ventilator did its work.

Frank was wracked with guilt. Why hadn't he gone into the house to say goodnight to the Senator? Why hadn't he kept Michael safe? Why hadn't he kept them all safe? "Tommy," he said, "I'm so sorry."

"You saved him, Frank. They thought he was dead, and if he'd lain there much longer, he would have been. If you hadn't noticed he would surely be gone. You saved him. How did you know? How could they not?"

"It was... I'm sorry, Tommy. It was a horrific scene. It was an honest mistake that they didn't realize he was alive. His pulse was so weak as to be almost undetectable, and he was covered in blood. And there were the others to check. And the children. Emotions were running high. It was a fluke that I noticed, really. I crouched down next to him and spoke his name. I told him I was sorry and his eyelids fluttered. Luckily there were still some EMTs on site and they raced in and got the chest tubes placed."

"We'll never be able to thank you enough, Frank, for keeping our brother alive."

Now the guilt came in huge waves, but Frank Malone was not a man who thought of his own needs first. Michael was getting the best of care, and there was nothing Frank could do for him. He would hunt down the evil men who had done this and make them pay.

CHAPTER TEN

BIRTHDAY

When the twins turned twenty-eight, Matt took Caroline on a cruise to celebrate, while his parents watched their kids at their home in Portland. Michael had a week off, and spent it at his parents' beach house. As usual, though, most of his time was spent down the beach with Lisa and David and their family.

Michael and his 16-year-old niece, Jessica, were kindred spirits. They both loved books and writing and music, and they whiled away happy hours practicing duets, Michael on the piano and Jessica playing her cello. Often Jess's friends were scattered around the house, and sometimes they brought their musical instruments and played along. At other times, when the kids were watching videos, swimming in the pool, or playing volleyball on the beach, Michael would read by the pool or write on his laptop. If he really needed to concentrate, he would escape to the quiet of his mother's beautiful sun porch, where he also said daily Mass for the family. It was an idyllic vacation.

On Saturday afternoon, the actual day of his birthday, Michael was reading by the pool while Lisa and David swam with their kids. Jess's friend, Hannah, and a couple of high school boys were there as well. Lisa's 14-year-old son, Beau, yelled, "Hey, Uncle Michael. Come and play chicken. I'll even let you have Georgie and I'll take Tyler, being as you're such an old man." 4-year-old Georgie and 6-year-old Tyler started to cheer. Michael laughed, stood up, and took off the t-shirt he was wearing with his swim trunks, just as the Senator and Mrs. Wallace stepped onto the patio.

"Happy birthday, sweetie," said his mom, kissing his cheek.

"Michael. Put a shirt on," said his dad.

Michael looked at the Senator in confusion. "I'm going swimming, dad," he said.

"Then put on one of those swim shirts."

"I'm not going to get burned, dad. I'm already kind of tan."

"That's not the point, Michael."

Michael slowly turned and faced the Senator. "What is the point? Sir."

The Senator stepped closer and spoke very quietly. "There are teenaged girls in the pool."

Michael felt anger bubbling up. "David doesn't have a shirt on, SIR, and nor does anyone else."

"David is a married man and a dad. You... you're... It doesn't look right. You have to consider these things now. And while we're on the subject, you spend way too much time with Jessica. You need to think, Michael. Think and be careful."

"What the hell are you implying? She. is. my. niece."

The Senator angrily answered his son. "I'm not implying anything. I'm just saying it doesn't look right. These are difficult times. I'm trying to protect your reputation, Michael."

Michael shot back. "My reputation? Or yours?" Then, as the Senator glared at him, he put on his shirt, sat down, and started lacing up his running shoes.

Beau called out, "Uncle Mikey. What are you doing? Come and swim."

Controlling his voice, Michael answered, "Sorry Beau. Another time. I'm going for a run. I need to clear my head."

Jessica and her best friend, Hannah, swam over to the side of the pool. "Can we come running with you?"

"Not this time, Jess." And he took off down the beach.

By the time he'd run the five miles into town he was tired and sweaty. He'd already walked into The Lucky Duck Tavern before he realized that he had neither phone nor wallet with him. Charlie, a good friend from high school, owned the bar now and was serving customers.

"Well, as I live and breathe, look what the wind blew in. Mikey Wallace. How's it going? What are you doing here? I thought Joe said that today was your birthday and there was some big party at the house."

"Hey, Charlie. Listen. Do you think you could spot me a bourbon neat? I don't have my wallet with me, but you know I'm good for it."

"On the house, Mikey. It's good to see you. Happy birthday."

Michael gulped down the drink like a man dying of thirst. "How about another one?"

Charlie studied him. "What's going on, Bubba?"

"Oh, you know."

"The old man on your case?"

Michael sighed. "Always."

Two bourbons later the door opened and Julie Conway walked into the bar. Charlie looked from her to Michael. "Man, Bubba. This is not your day."

Julie walked to the other side of the bar and looked at Charlie. "Set my friend over there up with another one on me, Charlie."

Michael stood up to leave.

Julie said, "You're not gonna accept it, Mikey? Sit down and have a drink and listen to a song. I think you owe me that much."

Michael and Julie had been a couple through their last year of high school and their first of college. When he realized he was being called to enter the seminary their breakup had hurt them both. And now Julie seemed to want to vent her anger. She walked to the jukebox and pushed a button. Lady Gaga started belting out "I'll Never Love Again." Michael downed his fourth bourbon and, with tears in his eyes, got up and slammed out of the bar.

Mark Simmons walked in a minute later. "Hey, Charlie. What are you serving in this rat hole? I just saw Mikey Wallace heaving his guts out in the parking lot."

"Nice going, Julie," said Charlie. "First the Senator is on his back and then you pull that crap. And today's his birthday."

Julie walked out to the parking lot and found Michael sitting on the bench of a nearby picnic table. She sat down next to him. "Want a cigarette?"

"I don't smoke."

"I know."

"Yeah. I'll take one."

They smoked in silence for a few minutes. "I'm so sorry, Mikey. It was a shock seeing you in The Duck. I'm having a bad day, and I took it out on you. I guess I wanted to hurt you, because my hurt from all those years ago came bubbling back up."

"Well, mission accomplished, Jules. Did it make you feel better?"

"No. It made me feel awful. Hurting people isn't what it's cracked up to be."

"Yeah. I know the feeling."

"Aww, Bubba," she sighed. "How come the very best ones always leave me?"

"You deserve way better than me, Jules," he answered quietly.

She handed him a tissue. "Come on, kiddo. Wipe off your face. I'll give you a ride home."

The picnic on the beach that night was subdued. Even the kids weren't as wild as usual. His favorite lemon cake tasted like cotton in his mouth, but he thanked his mom for making it. It was his worst birthday ever.

CHAPTER ELEVEN

WAKING UP

February 27 Michael

Pain. Voices. Bright lights. Somebody holding his arm. Caroline screaming. Maddie on the kitchen floor. Blood. Just a baby. Have to get up. Make them stop. Oh, dear God, the pain. Mom on the dining room floor, her body wrapped around little Anne, trying to protect her. So much blood. Dad's eyes are open. Can he see? Caro screaming. So much blood. Get up. Make them stop. Can't breathe. She's crying. Stop.

****

Thomas

They had taken Michael off the ventilator earlier that morning, but he was still in critical condition, and would need several more surgeries. He hadn't moved a muscle in a week, but they had eased back on the sedation medication, and Michael's eyes seemed to be moving behind closed lids. Thomas was hoping beyond all hope that he would wake up today. A nurse gently pulled back the blanket in order to check one of his chest tubes when without warning Michael started thrashing wildly around. He raised his broken arms up in front of his face and then flailed them around. He kicked with his left leg. His right leg was in a long brace, but he tried to kick with that one as well. The nurse, taken by surprise, got smacked in the face by one of Michael's arm braces.

Thomas flew to the bedside. He tried to sound calm and comforting as he pinned one of Michael's arms to the bed. Lisa, Kelly, and Joe, who had arrived at the hospital earlier in the week jumped in to help restrain him.

Michael was gasping for air and fighting as hard as his weakened body would let him. His eyes remained closed and he swung his head from side to side. "Stop. Don't." His voice was raspy and hoarse, barely above a whisper.

"Mikey," said Thomas. "It's ok. It's over. You're in the hospital. You're safe. It's ok."

Michael did not stop thrashing. One of his IVs started to pull loose. A bit of blood appeared around his left chest tube.

"It's Tommy," said Thomas, trying again. "Open your eyes. We're all here with you. Lisa and Kelly and Joe are here. It's ok. You're safe."

Michael frantically pulled his arms away. An IV popped out spurting blood.

Thomas let go of his arm, which left it free to flail around, hitting Tommy in the head. Ignoring the pummeling he was getting, he put one hand on either side of Michael's face, and turned it toward him. He leaned in close and shouted, "Michael Joseph! Look at me!"

Michael froze. His eyes blinked open.

Lisa spoke to him gently then, "Mikey? Are you awake?"

He turned his face toward her and tried to focus. "Mom?"

"No, sweetie. It's Lisa. Tommy and Kelly and Joe and I are here with you."

Michael closed his eyes. "Mom. Blood."

He opened his eyes again, struggling to wake up, and turned his head toward Thomas.

Tommy lowered his voice, "It's me, Bubba. It's Tommy. It's ok. You're safe."

Michael whispered, "T?"

"Yes," said Thomas, relieved that his brother had recognized him.

But Michael became agitated again and tried to sit up. His words were slurred and hard to make out as he rasped in a hoarse voice, "T! We need to go. Caro. Crying. Hurting her. Go get her, T! Hurry. They're hurting her. We have to go get her. She's crying."

"No, Bubba. No." Thomas gently pushed his brother back down onto the pillows and held him there. "It's all over. Nobody is crying. It's over. You're in the hospital."

Michael struggled against Thomas's arms. "I hear her. She's crying. They're hurting her. I have to get up. There's blood. I can't breathe. Maddie. Mom." He collapsed back against the bed. Tears rolled down his cheeks. His voice was almost gone.

Lisa brushed back the damp curls that had fallen over his forehead. "Mikey. Sweetie. It's over. I'm so sorry for what you went through. You're in the hospital. You've been here for more than a week. It's all over. You're safe."

But as it turned out, he wasn't.

CHAPTER TWELVE

PAUL

The murder of a United States Senator had law enforcement offices all over the country scrambling. The horrific addition of the murder of his family added to the frenzy. Agents sifted through email and paper letters. They tracked the writers of both. They checked on people recently released from prison who had a beef against the Senator. They studied various groups with opposing viewpoints to Senator Wallace and monitored social media complaints. It was like looking for a needle in a haystack. What if these guys hadn't written a letter or an email or even mouthed off about some perceived injustice? What if they'd just held onto their anger until it overflowed? There was little to no physical evidence. The attackers had apparently worn gloves and taken their weapons away with them. A rush had been put on the blood work and experts in blood spatter had brought in. FBI profilers were working with what little evidence they had. A great deal of hope was put into what they could learn from the eyewitnesses. Matthew Carter, Paul Carter, and Michael Wallace were the only survivors of the horrible attack.

Frank Malone still had some very good friends in the Bureau. They could understand his passion, and were willing to let him unofficially participate in some parts of the investigation. He knew the family well and could offer some insight into the family dynamics. He could help them put witnesses at ease.

Technically, Frank could not be faulted for doing a poor job. He made sure that Michael Wallace was safely inside the house, even though he was off duty at that point. His partner was supposed to be inside the house with the Senator and his family. These facts did not assuage Frank's conscience. The Senator had died. His assignment that evening had been to keep Michael Wallace safe. He had failed.

Frank wasn't allowed in all of the meetings, and couldn't see all of the paperwork, but he could go along with Agent Tierney and Agent Chase on the interviews of Matthew Carter and his son Paul. They were the only eye witnesses besides Michael Wallace, and Mikey was just regaining consciousness after a week in a coma. The family had been extremely protective of these survivors and this was the first they'd been able to talk to them. It was frustrating. They needed information right away, but the survivors were all seriously injured. Samantha Tierney felt that Frank would be a good liaison with Matt and Paul, as he had known them for years.

They gave Frank the lead with Paul who, with his father, was recuperating at his grandparent's house. Grandma and Grandpa Carter had been loath to let them in the door, and hovered anxiously nearby.

"Hi, Paulie. Do you remember me?"

"You're Frank. You work for my grandpa."

"That's right. Listen, Paul. We know you're a big boy, and you've been very brave. We need to ask you some questions about the night those bad men were in your house."

Paul's eyes filled with tears.

"Do you think you can do that, Paulie? Do you think you can answer some questions and help us catch the bad guys?"

Paul nodded and put his thumb in his mouth.

"Ok. First of all. How many bad men did you see in your house?"

"Two." Paul held up two fingers almost like a toddler.

"Good job remembering. Did you know the guys?"

"No." Paul frowned. "They had funny faces."

"Like masks?"

"Funny. Smushed. Their faces were weird."

"Paul. Do you know what a nylon stocking is?"

"No."

"Did your mom used to wear socks that you could kind of see through when she got dressed up for church on Sundays."

"Oh. Yeah."

"Paulie, do you think the guys were wearing socks like that over their heads?"

Paul sat up. "Yeah. They were. The funny socks smooshed up their faces!"

"Paul, were you in the family room that night?"

"I. I. I don't know. I was sleeping? And then I woke up? And my arm hurted. And they were hurting Mommy. Two guys."

Frank asked gently, "And who else did you see in the family room when you woke up?"

Paul wrinkled his forehead as he thought and said slowly, "My mommy, my daddy, Grandpa, and Uncle Mikey. Grandpa was sleeping on the floor. Uncle Mikey was lying on the floor, too, but he wasn't sleeping. He was trying to grab a bad guy by the leg. The guys were hurting my mommy." He teared up again.

"And what did you do then?"

"I runned over to Mrs. Fleming's house. I told her to call 911. That's what you do when you need help. 911. I learned that at preschool."

Paul started to cry in earnest then, and his grandparents ended the session before they could ask him anything more.

****

Samantha Tierney turned on the recorder and spoke into it stating the date and the names of the people present.

"Professor Carter? Do you mind if Frank Malone sits in on our session?"

"Not at all. He's a friend of the family. I'll take all the help I can get in finding out who did these horrible things to my family." Matt's arm was in a sling and there were greenish purple bruises around his eye and mouth. Bruised ribs and a lung that had been collapsed made him walk a bit hunched over.

"Thank you, Professor."

"It's ok to call me Matt."

"Thank you, Matt. This is just a preliminary session to get some basic facts down. We're also going to want to take you minute by minute through that night. I know it will be grueling for you, but it's necessary. And we'll want to do that while the facts are still fresh in your mind."

"I understand. And I'll do anything I can to help." Matt started to cry.

"Matt, how many people were in your house that night? Committing this crime, I mean, not your family or employees."

"There were two guys. It doesn't seem possible, does it? That two guys could do all that damage. But they took us by surprise, and they moved so quickly…"

"Let's take this a little slower. Did the guys have weapons?"

"Yes. They had… Well, they had knives, and iron bars. Like pokers? But without the pointed ends. Just long iron bars."

"And when did you first realize something was wrong?"

"I heard my mother-in-law scream. And then I heard feet running. It sounded like somebody ran from the kitchen into the dining room. And I jumped up and then I heard a moan. I don't know. It all happened so fast."

"And you were in the family room at this time?"

"Yes. Caroline and I and Paul and my father-in-law were in the family room." He sniffled.

"Where were your other children?"

"The girls were in the kitchen with my mother-in-law getting a snack. I think Greg had gone up to his room to play a video game."

"And your father-in-law's bodyguard? Where was he?"

"Gerry? I don't know. I think maybe he'd gone outside to check on a noise? I can't remember. I'm not sure."

"And then what happened? After you jumped up?"

"These two guys just came bursting into the room. One of them hit Paulie in the arm with the iron rod and Paul went slamming into the wall and then fell on the floor and was still. Caroline started screaming. The other guy grabbed my father-in-law by the hair and just viciously slit his throat. It happened so quickly. I felt like I was made of stone. I couldn't move. Then I guess somebody hit me on the head because I don't remember anything after that, until I woke up in the hospital."

"And where was your brother-in-law, Michael?"

"Mikey? He wasn't there."

"He wasn't in the family room with you?"

"No. He was still at the church. I mean, I guess he must have come in at some point because he got hurt, but I didn't see him there before I got knocked out."

"Did you recognize the two men?"

"No. They had stockings over their heads. But even so, no. I didn't recognize them."

As they walked to the door Matt asked Frank if he had been to see Michael in the hospital.

"Not since that first day. Have you?"

"No. But I've been talking to Tommy on the phone every day."

"Same," said Frank.

"I wonder if he'll ever wake up. I wonder if he'll even make it."

Frank turned to him in surprise. "I guess you haven't talked to Tommy yet today. Michael woke up this morning. He was confused, but definitely recognized the family."

"Oh, thank God," said Matt. "I know I should get over and see him. I should have gone before now. I just feel so helpless. And I can't leave Paul. He keeps asking about Mikey but I'm afraid if I take him to the hospital all the medical equipment will scare him. And Michael looks so much like Caroline. I worry that it would upset Paulie more to see him. Frank? Could Mikey shed any more light on what happened? Did he describe those guys?"

"No. He's barely awake and seems very confused about where he even is at this point. Nobody wants to risk questioning him until he's more fully conscious."

"Well, at least that gives us something to hope for, Frank. Paul and I and my parents pray for his recovery every night."

CHAPTER THIRTEEN

QUESTIONS

Frank tried to give the Wallace siblings privacy but continued to call Thomas every day for an update. The investigators were extremely anxious to interview Michael, and now that he was awake, they could not be held off. Thomas tried to stall them.

Frank Malone, Samantha Tierney, and Carl Chase did not call ahead to warn him this time. They simply appeared in the hall walking toward Michael's room. Thomas met them at the door. "He's not ready," Thomas told Frank. "He's barely awake. He's confused."

"They have to talk to him, Tommy," Frank told him. "Just a few questions. They'll won't push him."

"No. He doesn't know where he is half the time. Sometimes he thinks it's still happening. We can't do anything that might make it worse for him."

"Dr. Wallace," said Agent Tierney, "You do want to help us catch whoever did these terrible things to your family, don't you?"

"You know what? Not at the cost of my brother's health."

"Please. Just let us see how he is today. One or two questions if he's up to it."

And in the end, he knew that eventually he had to give them access to Michael. They filed quietly into the dim room where Michael dozed. As if sensing their presence, he stirred and his eyes fluttered open.

"Frank," he said in that quiet raspy voice.

"I'm so relieved to see you awake, Michael," said Frank. "This is Agent Tierney. And this is Agent Chase. They need to ask you a few questions about what happened the night of the attack. I'm really sorry, but it's important."

"Michael," began Agent Tierney.

"Father Michael," growled Tommy. He was constantly on the verge of picking a fight these days. "Show him some respect."

"I'm very sorry," said Agent Tierney, unflustered. "I certainly didn't mean any disrespect. Father Michael, we just need the answer to a couple of key questions, if you don't mind."

Michael rasped, "I'll try. So sleepy. Is it nighttime?" His eyelids drooped.

"No," said Samantha gently. "It's 2:00 in the afternooon. Father Michael. Can you tell me how many people attacked your family that night?"

Michael struggled to open his eyes. "Three," he whispered.

"Three?" asked Agent Chase, not quite able to cover his surprise. "Are you sure there were three?"

"Three," said Michael again. "Three guys."

Thomas was exasperated. "Can't you ask Matt these questions? And Paul? I know Paulie is young, but he's very precocious. I'm sure he can answer some questions."

"Yes, sir," said Agent Tierney. "And we have. It's important to verify the facts by finding out if the eyewitnesses saw the same things. And it's also important because Michael – excuse me, Father Michael – might have seen something that Mr. Carter and his son didn't."

Agent Chase asked, "Father Michael, where did you see these three people? Did you see one of them outside and the other two inside the house?"

"Three guys," said Michael. "Inside. Two hurting Caro. One hurting me." He could not keep his eyes open any longer and fell asleep.

****

Frank, Samantha, and Carl were drinking very bad coffee in the hospital cafeteria.

"Matt Carter says there were two guys. The kid says there were two guys. That makes it complicated. I'd be ok with the theory that Carter has something to hide. The mere fact that he was the least injured of anybody in that house except for Paul puts up a red flag. But I don't think a 4-year-old would be in on any conspiracy theory. And Carter did have some painful and serious injuries," said Carl. "Father Michael got it wrong."

"He's a pretty smart guy," said Frank. "And he's a guy who makes his living being careful with words."

"He's traumatized, drugged, and in pain," said Samantha. "He got it wrong. Or maybe the third guy came in after Matt Carter was knocked unconscious."

"But then there's Paul," said Carl. "He said there were two guys. He said uncle Mikey was lying on the floor. Matt Carter says he wasn't there."

"Maybe the third guy came in after Matt was unconscious and after Paul had run out of the house? Was Matt unconscious when Paul left? I wish we could have questioned the boy longer. Maybe the third guy had been outside dispatching Mr. Pelton," mused Samantha.

Carl said, "The police were there within minutes of Mrs. Fleming's 911 call. They knew the Senator was staying with his daughter and they didn't waste any time. I guess it's possible that a third guy ran into the house after Paul left and after Matt was knocked out, beat the shit out of Michael, and then ran out with his two buddies. But something definitely doesn't feel right."

"So, you think somebody is lying?"

"Not Michael," put in Frank.

"You may have some insight, but you're too close to the family, Frank. Is it possible that he's twisting the facts for some reason? Trying to confuse the issue? Hiding something? What was his relationship with his dad?"

"Listen. Michael and his dad had issues. The Senator had expectations through the roof and was really hard on him from the time he was small. He started out as his dad's favorite. But then his dad wanted him to go into politics. Maybe become President. Michael defied him and became a priest. After that the Senator got bitter and rode him even harder. In his eyes Michael couldn't do anything right. He turned into an adult who is way too hard on himself and has a giant case of anxiety. Big deal. If everyone who grew up with anxiety killed their parents there wouldn't be a soul left on the face of the earth. And besides, everybody had issues with the Senator. He was a difficult man. But Michael Wallace is the best man I've ever known and there is no way he is involved in this. And that's not even mentioning the fact that he's been knocking at death's door for the last week. No way. They're all confused. Or traumatized. Or just bad witnesses. You know how often witnesses get it wrong."

"These people weren't just casual observers, Frank. They were in the thick of it. Something is not right. Every scrap of information we've followed has led to a dead end. If the Senator was such a S.O.B. to his family, what about the siblings? Murder for hire?"

"No," said Frank. "Not a chance. He wasn't any more an S.O.B. than lots of guys who don't get murdered. I mean at the furthest stretches of the imagination maybe, maybe the Senator. But I know these people well. None of them would have hurt Mrs. Wallace. Or Caroline. Or the kids. Hell, none of them would have hurt the Senator. There is no way that any of them are involved."

CHAPTER FOURTEEN

THE ZOO

It was unheard of for Michael to get time off at Christmas, but this year Caroline and Matt and the children were coming to the beach for a week, and he was able to take a week off, thanks to the generosity of two of his priest friends who offered to help out at his parish. At around 10:00 on the second morning Caroline found him sleeping on the couch in the TV room, which was odd. He rarely napped.

"Wake up, goofball," she said, shaking his shoulder. "You and I and 6 or so children are going to the zoo."

He sat up. "What?" he said drowsily.

She looked at him more closely. He had dark circles under his eyes and a pinched look. "Oh, damn. Your ulcer is acting up."

"No. It was in the night, but I'm ok now. Just tired."

"You wouldn't lie to me, would you?"

"No. Well, yes. But I'm not lying right now. I feel fine."

"Go back to sleep, sweetie. I'm perfectly capable of wrangling a few children."

"No. I want to go. I've been dying to spend some time with the kids. Just give me 20 minutes to shower and wake up, and I'll be raring to go. Where's Matt?"

"Not going. He says he has work to do."

With Michael, Caroline, her three children and Lisa's 5, there were ten of them, so they had to take two cars. Tiny Paul and Georgie rode in strollers. Jessica and Beau said they were coming to help with the little ones, but they thoroughly enjoyed the zoo. Few things made Michael happier than being with his family. He loved his nieces and nephews deeply, and they felt the same about him.

At the lion exhibit Annie said, "Pick me up, Uncle Mikey. I can't see." In spite of his stomach pain (he had lied to Caroline after all) he hoisted her onto her shoulders. The other four smaller children began clamoring for a turn, as the babies looked on from their strollers.

"I'll make a deal with you," said Michael. "I'm very old and can't do this all day. But I'll give each of you one turn. You choose the exhibit where you want to ride on my shoulders."

"Oh, Bubba," said Caroline. "You don't have to. And, by the way, I'm wise to the fact that you lied to me this morning."

He winked at her as the children started negotiating.

"I want the giraffes."

"Ok, but I want the elephants."

They stopped for lunch and Caroline gave him a sideways glance when he said he wasn't hungry and just sipped slowly on a carton of milk.

Later, at home, they played board games while the smallest children napped. Michael lay on the floor in front of the fire and read to some of the children, and they to him. And then they sat around the big dining room table decorating the Christmas cookies that Catherine had made the previous day.

The weather was cool, but not freezing, so that night they donned their jackets and had a picnic on the beach and a bonfire. The adults and older children played volleyball. Michael was animated with the children, but when they weren't nearby he grew quiet.

Sitting in a beach chair next to him late that evening, enjoying the sound of the waves, Catherine said, "I hope you don't mind me saying this, son, but you would have made a wonderful dad."

Michael looked at her. "That was the hardest thing to give up. But look at it this way, Mom. Now I have bunches of kids and can hand them off when they need clean diapers."

She laughed and took his hand. "Thank you for giving the kids a lovely time today, though. I know it was hard for you."

"What? No it wasn't. I enjoyed every minute of it."

"Honey, I know you're hurting."

He waved his hand at her. "Mom, it was a perfect day. It wasn't hard for me. Stop worrying."

"Still, I hope you'll take some medication and get a good night's sleep."

"Yes, ma'am." He squeezed her hand. "I'm fine, mom. Really."

Caroline came up behind them and slapped the back of his head playfully. "Spoiled brat!"

Michael reach back and half-heartedly tried hit her as she ducked away. "Witch!"

"Language, Michael Joseph," said Catherine absentmindedly.

Michael laughed. "I said witch, mom, not bitch."

"Michael!"

"Ok. Sorry." And then to Caroline, "Stop horning in on my mom time."

Catherine sighed. "Here we go again." But she was smiling. She loved every moment of having her wonderful, difficult, kind, bickering twins together.

CHAPTER FIFTEEN

NOT SO CONSCIOUS

All he needed was five minutes in that room. But the brothers and sisters took turns staying overnight and the priest was never alone. He supposed he could do two of them, but at this point it would be better if it looked like the priest just died from his injuries, or it was an accident. And he'd been told that it had to happen soon. And he was getting tired of watching.

****

"Well, hi there."

Michael looked up at the nurse standing over him. "Hi."

"It's nice to see you awake. My name is Jackie, and I've been one of the nurses taking care of you. Can you tell me your name?"

"Isn't it written on that chart?"

"Oh, a comedian. Yes, it is. And, yes, I know your name. But I have to see if you know it, and then I have to ask you a bunch of silly questions to judge your state of consciousness."

"My name is Michael."

"Michael what?"

"Michael Joseph Ignatius Wallace," he said. "How's that for being conscious?"

"Ignatius?"

"Ignatius. You can look it up if you want, or ask my brother."

"I don't have to look it up. It's in the chart."

Michael chuckled and then grimaced. The slightest movement sent a wave of pain through his chest.

Trying to get his mind off of it he asked, "Want me to tell you about St. Ignatius?"

"Yes."

"He. His leg was. Um. He was..." He searched his memory. Ignatius was his Confirmation Saint. He loved this story and knew it well. Why wouldn't the words come out?

"How about we save that story for later. How old are you, Michael Joseph Ignatius?"

This question also gave him pause and his smile faltered. "How old? Um. It was our birthday. I'm. I. I can't seem to think."

"That's fine. You had a pretty bad bump on the head and you've been unconscious for a while. It may take you a bit of time to remember things. You're 30 years old. Can you tell me where you are right now?"

He looked around the room "In a hospital."

"And why are you in the hospital?"

"I'm sick? Or hurt. Or something. Oh," his face fell. "There were some guys hurting us."

"Do you know where this hospital is?"

"Wilmington? But, no. We were. We were visiting Caro. I can't seem to remember the name of the city." He looked at her. "I guess I'm not quite as conscious as I thought."

"It's ok. You're doing fine. You're in Portland."

He was getting tired which made him all the more confused. "Caroline lives in Portland. But why are my brothers and sisters here?"

"They flew out to be with you after you got hurt. I think we'll stop with the questions for now and let you get some rest. Is there anything I can do to make you more comfortable?"

"No. Thank you. I feel really tired and foggy. Is my brother, Tommy here?"

"They went down to get some dinner. Oh, here they come now."

****

As Jackie left the room and Michael's siblings entered she noticed an orderly pushing a cart down the hall. She'd seen him around recently, but didn't know who he was.

"Can I help you find a room?" she asked him.

"Oh, no thanks," he said. "I think I'm on the wrong floor. I'm new and they send me all over delivering things. Low guy on the totem pole, you know." He turned and headed for the door.

She laughed, "Ok. Well let me know if you need help."

CHAPTER SIXTEEN

CAKE FACE

Joe

He was a later bloomer. But by his Junior year in high school things started to click for Joseph Wallace. He graduated with a halfway decent grade point average and, after a stint at the community college, got accepted into The University of North Carolina where Joe, out from under the intense scrutiny of his father, flourished. Then he went on to Law school, married his lovely wife Sara, and settled down to raise his family. Another man might have resented his brothers and sisters for their early successes and the pressure it added to his life, but that was not who Joe Wallace was. He loved them all passionately.

Joe was used to sitting back and letting his siblings take charge. The family seldom asked for his opinion or help. But they enjoyed his company and he theirs. Today, for the first time in his life Jo-Jo, out of all of them, was the one his baby brother needed the most.

Michael had had a rough night after the latest surgery on his chest. The pain was intense, but it was more than that. He seemed to be fighting sleep, like a toddler who was exhausted but didn't want to close his eyes. He moved restlessly on the bed. His eyes would droop and then snap open again. Joe sat at his side while the others talked quietly across the room.

"Go to sleep, Bubba." Joe told him gently. "Sleep away some of the pain."

"I can't, Joey."

"Sure you can. You're so tired. I'll sit right here with you. Go to sleep, Mikey."

Michael continued to toss and turn uncomfortably.

"Do you want me to call the nurse? Do you need some pain meds?"

"No. I just. I can't. I just don't want to close my eyes."

"Tell me, Bubba, please. What's on your mind? What is it? We all love you. Give us the gift of sharing your pain."

Michael started to cry softly. "Jo-Jo? Every time I close my eyes, I see her. Maddie. Lying on the kitchen floor with her neck sliced open. She was so tiny, Joe." He sobbed. "I walked around the kitchen island, and there she was. She had on those pink pajamas with the unicorns. The ones I gave her for Christmas. But they were all red. And her hair...."

Thomas and Lisa and Kelly froze across the room. They were paralyzed with their own grief, and their hearts broke for Michael because of what he had witnessed.

"You want to know the worst part, Joey? I can't remember what she looked like. Every time I close my eyes, I see her all covered in blood. I can't see her the way she was before. I don't remember what she looked like."

Joe wanted to hold his brother, but there were too many ways to hurt him. So many wires and tubes. So many injuries. He reached over and stroked Michael's shoulder.

"Listen to me, Mikey. I'm going to tell you a story. Close your eyes."

"I can't."

"You can. Close your eyes, Bubba, and listen to me. I want you to think of your birthday party. Yours and Caroline's. This last one, just a few months ago."

"Joe. No."

"Yes. Don't interrupt. Close your eyes and listen. You weren't supposed to be there. You were giving a talk. But at the last minute something got canceled and you surprised us. Remember? Caro and Matt and the kids were all there. Everybody was. You walked in the door and the whole place erupted. We were so happy to see you. Maddie came running up screaming, 'Uncle Mikey!' and you dropped your bags and knelt down and hugged her."

"Joe. Don't. I can't."

"Shh. Listen. But before I can go on, I need to remind you of something. Because your ridiculous obsessiveness about clean shirts is part of this story. How many times have one of us said, 'Oh, for God's sake, Michael. You dropped one crumb on that shirt. You'd need a magnifying glass to see where it landed,' But you'd pick at it, and brush at it, and pull at it, until you finally couldn't stand it, and you'd go up and change. You're really a very annoying man, Michael."

Michael sniffed. "There's nothing wrong with a clean shirt, Joe."

"Not unless you're pathologically obsessed with clean shirts. But anyway. Hush. This is my story. So Maddie had been eating chocolate cake and ice cream and had it all over her face. And she wouldn't let anybody clean her up. All the adults kept swiping half-heartedly at her with wash cloths, but she was having none of it. You know what a terror she was. Just like Caro. If that child did not want her face washed, she was not going to have her face washed. When she hugged you, she got cake and goo all over the front of your shirt. It wasn't just a crumb. It was a huge mess, and we all thought you were going to have a stroke. But there was Maddie, demanding, 'Read to me, Uncle Mikey.' And instead of racing off to change your shirt the way you usually did, you picked her up and grabbed a book off the coffee table and plopped her on your lap in the rocking chair. Remember, Mikey?"

"Joey, please."

"You didn't even take time to say hello to everyone or grab a beer or have something to eat. The adults were trying to tell her to let you catch your breath and have some dinner. But you just held that baby and started to read as if nobody else was in the room. You used those funny voices that the little kids like so much, and she was absolutely beaming up at you with those big dark eyes. And she was haloed by those wild brown curls, just like Caro's. Just like yours. And her face was all smeared with cake and ice cream. Remember? Can you see her, Mikey? Can you see that little cake-face looking up at you?"

Michael closed his eyes. He whispered, "I see her, Jo-Jo."

"Ok, then. Whenever you need a picture in your head of our beautiful angel, I want you to close your eyes and see that little cake-face looking up at you. That's our Maddie. Little cake-face."

Michael slept. They all knew deep in their hearts that Joe was a hero. Sometimes they just needed to be reminded.

CHAPTER SEVENTEEN

DOUBTS

The FBI investigators returned to question him further, dropping in unannounced while Michael was in surgery, getting his shattered kneecap replaced. They sat with Thomas, Lisa, Joe, and Kelly and talked to them while they waited, getting some background information. They tried to make it sound like a casual conversation, but the siblings were wary. Still, they felt they had nothing to hide. They didn't see how it could help find those responsible for the attack, but they wanted to cooperate. All of the siblings agreed that their dad had been tough on them, especially on his youngest son. They readily admitted that Michael had been the favorite from the time he was a small child and it didn't seem to bother them at all. They gave off a "better him than me" vibe, but more than that, he seemed to be their favorite, too.

In some ways their childhood had been idyllic, they insisted. They lived in a beautiful house on the ocean with parents who doted on them. They were a close family. Grandparents, aunts, uncles, and cousins were in and out of their home. They were attractive and popular at school and had lots of friends. But the Senator's expectations had been a crushing burden on them all. They loved their dad, they said. He wanted the best for them. He was a good dad in lots of ways. He spent time with them, went to their school and sporting events, took them on vacations, talked to them. Things were fine, and even good, as long as you did exactly what the Senator wanted.

Michael, they said, was driven. To outsiders it seemed that he had a natural talent for just about anything he touched. But they saw how hard he worked and practiced. They all tried very hard to please their father, but none worked as hard at it as their younger brother. The Senator wanted him to pitch on his little league team. He spend countless hours practicing until he could throw a ball accurately. His interests were in books and music, but the Senator wanted him to play football as his older brothers had. So at fourteen Michael started lifting weights and working out and practicing. He was made quarterback in his sophomore year. He wanted to major in literature and philosophy, but the Senator wanted him to study political science and law. He did so. He excelled at both. Dad was happy.

In fact, the Senator had never been happier than he was sitting in a box seat at the college stadium surrounded by his friends watching Michael play football. He'd never been prouder. Michael maintained a 4.0 average and was probably going to set some school records on the field in a few years. But after his freshman year Michael announced that he wanted to stop studying law. He wanted to stop playing football. He wanted to switch schools. His flabbergasted father was furious. The Senator felt like this whole thing had been sprung on him suddenly. His son was walking away from an amazing life, and he was not about to let that happen. He didn't see how impossible he made it for his children to discuss goals that were not his own. And finally Michael got the courage to announce that he had decided to enter the seminary instead of becoming involved in the law or politics. That was when his relationship with his father really changed. The Senator had never been opposed by anyone in the family, at least not successfully. Michael never raised his voice. The Senator did. It seemed that the angrier and more demanding he got, the calmer and more reasonable Michael became. Of course, that was his outward demeanor. His ulcer began acting up almost constantly, and he lost weight. He didn't sleep. But the Senator finally, for the first time in his, life threw in the towel. After that things had slowly gotten calmer for the most part. His father seemed to enjoy the beautiful ceremony in the cathedral when Michael was ordained. Michael became a sought-after speaker. "Father Michael Wallace" didn't have the same ring to the Senator as "Senator Michael Wallace" or "President Michael Wallace", but dad had gone to a couple of Michael's talks recently and found he had a different reason to be proud. Michael and his father were enjoying a fragile peace in their relationship.

****

Once Michael was settled back in his hospital bed, the agents tried to talk to him. As the surgical anesthetic wore off he became more alert, but also seemed reticent and a bit more unsure than the last time they had questioned him.

"Father Michael, do you remember telling us that there were three attackers at your sister's house that night?"

"Yes," said Michael.

"And is that the way you still remember it?"

"Yes. I think. Yes. Three guys."

"You think there were three guys?"

"No. I'm um. I'm sure. I know there were three guys."

"Father Michael, do you think you could describe them to us?"

"They had stockings over their faces."

"What about height? Weight? Race? Hair color?

"They were. Um. One of them was about as tall as me. But heavier. One was shorter. I don't know. They were bending over Caro. They were white, I think. Dark hair, I think."

"And the third one?" This was the crux of the matter. They were really anxious for information about this mysterious third attacker, if there even was one.

"I. I don't know. I couldn't see him."

"You couldn't see him? But you're sure he exists?"

"Yes. Two guys were hurting Caro. They had stockings over their faces. The third guy... I was lying on the floor. I couldn't get up. My leg wouldn't work. I was dizzy. But the third guy was standing over me. He was stomping his foot on my chest, over and over again."

"Did the third guy have a stocking over his face as well?"

"I don't know. I couldn't see him."

"Do you remember anything about him? Clothing, size, voice? Anything at all?"

"I'm sorry. I'm trying, but no."

"Father Michael," said Samantha "We're trying to get a picture of what it was like. You were lying on the floor. Your kneecap had been shattered and you'd been hit in the head. Were you lying on your back?"

"Yes. I think so. Yes."

"So you were lying on the floor on your back. And a man was standing over you and stomping on your chest. And you couldn't see him? Couldn't you have just looked up to see him? Were your eyes open? I don't understand."

"I don't know. I don't understand it either. I can't remember."

"Father Michael, can you do something for us? Can you close your eyes and concentrate and think about lying on that floor and looking up at the guy? You don't have to remember the other things. Just look up in your mind at the guy standing over you. Can you see him at all?"

"Please," said Michael. "I can't remember. Can we stop? I feel so tired and light headed. I feel nauseated. I just can't talk about this anymore right now. Please. I can't remember."

"Just a few more minutes, please," said Carl.

All of the siblings were rattled and not thinking straight. Even the brief description Michael had given brought back the overwhelming feelings of grief and dread. Swimming up through the fog of misery Joe began to get an uncomfortable feeling. Michael had no legal counsel. Of course he hadn't done anything wrong, but Joe did not like the way these questions were being asked. Innocent people had been railroaded before, when the real suspects could not be found. And everyone was frantic to solve the murder of a sitting Senator. Joe berated himself. He was a lawyer, and he should have been more careful about protecting his brother. They were pushing Michael too hard, and both his physical and mental health were fragile. If Michael was driven further toward the brink who knows what he might say. Matt and Paul had both said there were two guys. Michael said there were three. Could his words be twisted and his story discounted because of his trauma? Did they suspect him of covering something up? Joe intervened. "I'm acting as my brother's attorney temporarily until we can hire other legal counsel. This session is over now."

"Mr. Wallace," said Agent Pierson, "We are not accusing your brother of anything. We're just trying to firm up some facts. Surely you want to help us get at the truth."

"Until we can arrange for legal counsel for Michael, this session is over," repeated Joe.

CHAPTER EIGHTEEN

LOST

Why did she say that? Caroline's last words to him replayed over and over in his head, and each time was worse than the last. It gnawed at him every time he was awake. She had known he couldn't save her. He'd always been the timid one, the weak one, the incapable one. People thought that he was strong. But they were wrong. She knew. Caroline knew that he was no hero. She proved that with those words. She knew he wasn't strong enough mentally or physically to save her. That would be his last memory of her - her acknowledgement that he was a failure. The words she spoke came to him again. They killed his spirit a little more each time he remembered them.

He slept and dreamed of that time so many years ago when he first realized that Caro was the strong one, the one who would always take care of him. They were six years old and still a bit spoiled and wild. Catherine had dressed the twins in adorable matching outfits and taken them to a park on the edge of a wooded area to get professional photos taken of her beautiful babies. The twins were crabby and uncooperative, which made the session last a long time. And the longer it lasted, the more sullen the twins became. Finally, it was over and Catherine went inside the log office to look at proofs on a computer screen. It was past dinner time, and the angry twins sulked by the door.

"I hate this dress," complained Caroline. "I want to put on shorts and go play."

"My sweater is itchy," added Michael. "I'm hot, and I'm sick of smiling."

Caroline had one of her usual inspired thoughts. "Let's run away."

Michael was doubtful. "Where?"

Caroline looked around the lovely field of flowers and at the inviting shade of the trees at the edge. "Come on," she said, and began running toward the woods.

Michael tore after his sister. They ran and ran, using up the energy they'd stored from sitting still for so many photo poses. Michael screeched to a halt when they came to a small river. "Don't go in there, Caro. If you get your good clothes wet, we'll be in trouble."

"Come on, chicken," she teased. "It's only knee deep. I thought you were hot and sweaty." She stepped into the water, dress shoes and all. "Oooh. It feels nice."

Michael hesitated a moment but then, as he always did, he followed his twin. They waded down the river for a while until they found a meandering path.

"Let's play hobbits," said Caroline. "I'll be Frodo." Their parents and older siblings had been reading Lord of the Rings to the twins at bedtime for a while now.

"Frodo's a boy," retorted Michael. "I'm Frodo. You have to be Galadriel."

"Frodo's a hobbit!" insisted Caroline. "Boy or girl doesn't matter. You can be Aragorn."

Michael thought about this. "Do I get to have a sword?"

"Of course, dummy. Aragon had Andúril. That's the best sword."

Michael picked up a stick and ran through the trees swinging it enthusiastically. "Don't call the king a dummy," he shouted. The twins ran deeper and deeper into the woods.

****

Catherine Wallace stepped outside to check on her rebellious youngest children. Michael and Caroline were nowhere to be seen. She frowned and called to them, but got no answer. Nervously she walked around the log building calling for the twins. The photographer and his assistant came outside and began calling the children's names as well. All was silent. They walked to the edge of the woods and shouted, but there was no reply. That's when the panic started to set in.

By the time Senator Wallace's young twins had been missing for three hours a whole contingent of police cars had arrived at the field. A helicopter flew over the woods. Lisa Wallace hurried to the site with the twins' pajamas for dogs to sniff, and they and their trainers set off into the woods, but the dogs lost the scent at a small river. The Senator and several FBI agents had arrived at the scene, along with various news vans. The more time that went by, the more the awful realization began to occur to everyone that this might not just be children wandering off, but an actual kidnapping. It was getting dark.

****

Michael heard a noise and looked up through the thick leaf cover above their heads. "Hey. Is that a helicopter? Cool. Caro, I'm hungry. Let's not run away anymore," he said. "I want to go back. Maybe that helicopter is giving rides." He was hot and dirty. His shoes and clothes stuck to him uncomfortably, and he wanted to go home.

"Don't be such a baby, Mikey," said Caroline. But she agreed that it was time to find their way back to the photo site.

They walked until sun set and the temperature dropped. Now both twins were hungry, cold, tired, and nervous. Mosquitos and black flies began biting them, and they could hear the rustlings of animals nearby. They wandered for what seemed like hours but couldn't find the little river or the pretty field with flowers where they'd sat for portraits earlier. They came to a hill that didn't look familiar but thought maybe if they climbed it they would be able to see where the pretty field was. It was totally dark now, and walking was scary. They came to a little scooped out area in the hill, almost a cave, and the exhausted twins sat down to rest. Michael started to cry.

"Don't worry, Bubba." His sister put her arm around him. "It will be ok. I'll take care of you. I'll never leave you. You can always count on me."

The tracking dogs found them sleeping in the cave with their arms around each other early the next morning.

The twins were rushed to the hospital, but other than being hungry, scared, and covered with bug bites, they were pronounced fine and sent home where they were bathed, fed, and smothered with hugs and kisses. They were grounded to their rooms for a week, but after seeing their adorable little bug-bit, repentant faces at dinner that night no one had the heart to enforce the punishment, and it fell by the wayside.

****

Michael woke from the dream. She promised she would never leave. But she had left. And her final words to him broke his heart.

CHAPTER NINETEEN

DEPRESSION

Michael was broken, and not just physically. They could all see that. He hadn't spoken a word about the attack since his breakdown over seeing Maddie on the kitchen floor and the questioning by the police. The more alert and conscious he became over the next few days the quieter he grew. He would lie in bed staring at the ceiling or out the window, and hours would go by without him saying a word. They were all suffering, of course, but it was different with Mikey. They would gather in a quiet circle and weep while he slept. Sometimes they would voice their deepest fears about what their loved ones had suffered. At other times they would tell stories about Mom and Dad and Caro and the kids that made them laugh.

"Remember when Annie and Greg brought that snake in the house to show mom?"

"Remember the birthday party when mom told Mikey to talk to dad about his balls?"

"Remember when the twins ran away?"

"Remember when Caro pushed dad into the pool? Only Caro would have had the guts."

It felt cathartic. Michael didn't participate in any of these discussions, and they didn't want to push him. His physical wounds and the heavy medication surely played a part in the change in his personality. But it was more than that. Thomas suspected that maybe he was even pretending to fall asleep when they tried to mention the ones they had lost in his presence. He answered their questions with a word or short phrase. And then he went back to staring. He was slipping away from them.

"How you doin', Bubba?"

"Good."

"Good? Seriously? Mikey, I don't believe I've ever seen anybody as far away from good as you are."

"I'm ok."

"Can I do anything to make you more comfortable?"

"No, thank you."

"Do you want to watch TV? Maybe a movie?"

"No, thanks."

"Do you want me to read to you?"

"Not right now, thanks."

And finally, in desperation, "Mikey. Please talk to me. Tell me what you're thinking. Tell me what you're feeling. Tell me anything. Please, Bubba. Let me in."

"Tommy. I. I shouldn't be here."

"I don't know what you mean."

"I mean I should be with them. Mom and dad and Caro and the kids. I was there with them. I belong with them. God should have taken me."

"Mikey, no. What are you saying? You belong here. God kept you here for a reason. We need you. Do you know what it would do to your sisters to hear you talk like this? Don't ever say that again. And don't think it. We can't lose you. You listen to me, Michael Joseph. You can't leave us. You just can't. We will not survive another loss. You have to promise me that you will keep fighting."

"Do you know what she said to me, Tommy?"

"What? Who? What who said to you, Bubba? Caro? Mom? What did she say to you?"

"Nothing. Never mind."

"Tell me, Bubba. Please."

"No. It's nothing."

He needed help. They felt they all needed counseling, but Michael most especially. They were becoming worried about the confusing answers he was giving police. They didn't suspect that he'd done anything wrong, but could he possibly know something that he didn't want to tell? He needed a lawyer. They had called their uncle, William Wallace, and asked him to represent Michael. Joe would stand in for Uncle Bill until they could get home.

Truth be told, the thing they wanted most was for him to confide in them. They were his brothers and sisters, and more than that, they had helped raise the twins. They felt that they were almost his surrogate parents. Surely he trusted them. But Mikey had always been very private about his feelings. He remained silent.

They kept trying. Wallace children did not give up easily. And finally, a few days later, "Bubba, can I do anything to make you more comfortable?"

"Can I brush my teeth?"

"Sure, sweetie. I'll find a toothbrush and help you."

"My hair feels dirty. And, Tommy? This gown has something on it. A spot of blood or something. Can I have a clean one?"

Thomas turned to his siblings and grinned. "He's back."

He wasn't though. Not really. Michel's siblings clung to this rare moment of normalcy and felt a bit of hope that their brother might survive the trauma he'd experienced. They realized that he was forever changed. They all were. But they longed for the day when Mikey would give them that crooked smile that always accompanied the mischief in his eyes. The smile that always seemed to win everyone over.

CHAPTER TWENTY

IN THE RECTORY

"Father, what on God's green earth are you doing?"

Michael flashed her his most winning smile. He had heard this question, or some variation of it, many times since moving into the new rectory two months ago.

"Um... grating carrots and cucumbers?"

"Have I not asked you to stay out of my kitchen?"

"You have, Mrs. Murphy."

"And how many times have I asked you that, Father Michael?"

"Many times, Mrs. Murphy. But, listen. I wanted to surprise you with this recipe I saw online." said Michael, sheepishly.

"Father? Many people grate things into a deep bowl so that they don't end up with bits of carrot and cucumber flying all over the kitchen."

"I'll clean it up. I promise. You won't even know I was ever in the kitchen." It was a promise he'd made before and kept with varying amounts of success. "And you'll have a delicious bowl of sesame peanut noodles with vegetables to boot."

"Sesame peanut noodles, my foot." Eleanor Murphy sighed loudly, picked up a cloth, and started cleaning the messy counter. Michael looked at her out of the corner of his eye and caught her smiling. Everybody was terrified of the redoubtable Mrs. Murphy. Michael had won her over in less than a week.

It started with a knock on his door on the day after he arrived.

"Father Michael? May I come in?"

"Sure. Come in."

"Father? What are you doing?"

"I'm, um, making the bed?" He'd dragged the vacuum cleaner out of the upstairs closet. "And then I was going to vacuum the carpet."

"You were going to what now?"

"Make the bed. And vacuum the carpet. I don't have any obligations as it's my first day, so I thought I'd tidy up and then maybe walk over to the school and meet some people."

Mrs. Murphy took in the immaculate room. After only one day his things were already unpacked and put neatly away. She frowned at him. "Cleaning is my job. Do you want me out on the streets with nothing to do and no way to earn a living?"

Michael looked at her in surprise. "But I thought your job was to cook for us. You do housekeeping chores, too?

Mrs. Murphy studied him. "Of course. It's been a rare occurrence for a priest in this rectory to make his own bed or tidy up his room. And not one of them has ever run the vacuum. I doubt they'd know how. To be honest, I've found most of your ilk to be... well, slobs."

Michael smiled. "They didn't have Catherine Wallace for a mother. Whenever there was a surprise inspection, woe be to the Wallace child with an untidy room."

"But it's not likely she'll be holding an inspection here, though, is it? Doesn't she live two or three hours away?"

Michael grinned. "That's where she's tricky. You just never know. Better safe than sorry."

And later that same afternoon. "Father Michael. What in the sam hill do you think you're doing?"

"I. Uh. Everybody is pretty busy today, so I thought I'd make some cookies. Lemon cookies. Lemon is my favorite flavor."

"And do you know how to make these lemon cookies?"

Michael shrugged.

She continued, "And do you know if we even have the necessary ingredients? And who's going to clean up your mess?"

"Well, but how hard can it be? Ingredients? Don't cookies have flour and sugar and stuff in them? And do we have any lemons?"

Mrs. Murphy glowered at him. "With all due respect, Father, you are to stay out of my kitchen. If you want cookies, I'll make them. Look. If you don't have anything to do today go find something you enjoy to keep yourself busy and out of my hair. What do you like to do?"

"I like to play the piano, and I like to read."

"Great. There's a piano in the front room. I'm sure you have plenty of books in your room. Go do one of those things. But first find me a recipe for those lemon cookies online and I'll make the blasted things for you."

"Can't I help? I'd really like to learn how to make them," said Michael, who had been making lemon cookies since he was 8 years old and knew the recipe by heart.

Mrs. Murphy heaved a sigh. "You're getting off on the wrong foot with me, Father."

Michael nodded. "Yes, I know. I'm terribly sorry. Unfortunately, I'm very annoying. My brothers and sisters tell me that all the time. I mean, I'll try to be less annoying, but I haven't had much success with that yet."

Mrs. Murphy blinked. "You haven't had much... Fine. Get the recipe. I'll let you measure some ingredients."

Michael carefully measured out the flour and sugar and then hopped up onto the counter and sat chatting with her while she finished the cookies, telling amusing stories about his family and asking about hers. Mrs. Murphy surprised herself by not scolding him for sitting on the counter. He tried to help with the dishes, but at that point she succeeded in shooing him out of the kitchen. She took a plate of cookies in to him and listened for a bit as he played the piano. He played beautifully. Surely there was no way he could have known that Pange Lingua Gloriosi was her favorite song. The cookies were delicious, and she added the recipe to her box of favorites.

By the time Michael had asked Mrs. Murphy to help him learn how to make deviled eggs, a recipe he'd mastered at 10, and chicken salad, one of his specialties at home, he had won her over.

Shortly thereafter Michael's became life very busy, and he rarely had time to stop by the kitchen for anything more than a quick hello. He had parish work to do, and was also sent out on numerous speaking engagements. But he brought her flowers on her birthday and always asked about her family. Mrs. Murphy worried about him as if he were her own son. He worked too hard and his meals were sporadic. He looked tired. He was too thin. When she asked if he didn't like her cooking, he had to admit that he had an ulcer which sometimes flared up and made it difficult for him to eat. She was careful, then, to make dishes that would be easy on his stomach. He laughed it off when she told him he looked tired.

"Mrs. Murphy? I love being a priest. And being assigned to this Parish has been a huge blessing in my life. If I'm tired it's a good tired. I couldn't be happier."

****

"Father Michael? Are you ok?"

Michael was sitting in a recliner in the rectory tv room. His computer was on his lap, but he was dozing. He looked up sleepily. "I'm ok, Mrs. Murphy."

"But you... Well, you look pale and you were grimacing."

"I'm having a little trouble with my ulcer today. It's fine. I'll be ok."

"Can I get you anything? Do you want some breakfast?"

"Decidedly not. But thank you. I've already taken some medication. It's my day off, so I'll just relax. Don't worry. I'll be fine."

The phone on the table next to his chair buzzed. It was the parish secretary. "Father, Michael? I'm sorry to bother you, but everyone else is out, and the hospital is calling for a priest to anoint one of our parishioners."

"Ok," sighed Michael. "Tell them I'll be there in 20 minutes." He went upstairs to change.

When he returned from the hospital, he was very white and was walking a bit hunched over.

Mrs. Murphy saw him and said, "Father, you need help."

"Mrs. Murphy, I've been dealing with this problem for twenty years. I'll take some more medication and sleep for a bit. Everything will be ok. Please don't worry."

A few minutes his brother, Tommy, called his cell phone. "What's up, Bubba?"

"Nothing. What's up with you?"

"Michael? Are you having a problem today?"

"Just a little flare up. I'll be ok."

"Have you thrown up?"

"Just a little bit, Tommy. And that was in the middle of the night."

"Was there blood?"

"Just a little. Listen, Tommy. I've taken my meds. I'm going to take a nap and I'll be fine."

"Are you lying to me?"

Michael didn't answer.

"I'm coming to get you. You may need to get that cauterized."

Michael hung up and walked into the kitchen.

"You called my brother."

"I. I'm sorry. I thought you needed help."

"Don't do that again." He'd never spoken to her with that cold tone in his voice before, and it disturbed her.

"Father, I'm sorry. Please don't be mad at me."

Michael turned and walked away.

Mrs. Murphy took Thomas up to Michael's room when he arrived. He knocked and then entered. She heard him say, "What the hell, Bubba? You sleep on a toddler bed in a closet?"

Michael sighed. "It's a perfectly normal room, Tommy. I don't need a palace. I just sleep here."

"But that bed. You can't even stretch out on it. Your legs must hang off the end."

"It's just a bed. People sleep on the ground."

"Yeah? Well, I'm going to buy you a bigger bed."

"Don't be ridiculous. If I need a bigger bed I can get one myself. This is fine."

After the cauterization Thomas wanted to take Michael back to his own home, but Michael wouldn't hear of it. So late in the night they returned to the rectory, and Thomas helped him into bed. After he left, Michael tossed and turned on the small, uncomfortable bed and finally took his pillow and blanket down to the tv room where he managed to doze in a recliner. Mrs. Murphy found him there the next morning.

Michael, usually fastidious about his appearance, was wearing flannel pajama pants and a wrinkled t-shirt. He was deathly pale. His cheeks and chin were covered in stubble, and his hair was wild. His eyes drooped from the residual effects of the anesthetic they'd given him before the cauterization. She'd never seen him look so disheveled and ill.

"Father Michael," she ventured. "Was your bed too uncomfortable?"

"No. I just couldn't sleep so I thought I'd come down here and watch a little TV."

"Well, I brought you some yogurt and a glass of milk. Your brother said you should try and eat a few bites of something with your medication." She continued, "I didn't call him. I promise. He called me this morning and asked me to check on you."

"Thank you, Mrs. Murphy," He said wearily. "Listen, I'm sorry for being cranky with you yesterday. I'm still not happy that you went behind my back like that. I'm an adult and have been dealing with this ulcer for years. But I'm not mad at you. I realize you did it because you care. I'll make a deal with you. I'll try to ask for help if I need it, and you try to wait until I ask."

"I'll try," she answered solemnly. But they both knew she wouldn't.

CHAPTER TWENTY-ONE

NOT AGAIN

It had to happen tonight, before the priest became alert enough to start remembering. He hadn't been able to get a weapon past the hospital metal detectors, but wasn't worried about overpowering a guy who'd been on a respirator and had multiple surgeries. If he had to take out one of the siblings with him, so be it. He was certainly capable of strangling one of those white-collar wimps.

****

Frank

He was so torn. He desperately wanted information so he could help the investigation. But he also wanted to be there for the Wallace kids the way he had in the past. For many, many years his job had been keeping the Senator safe, at home and on the various trips he took, both business and personal. Sometimes this included family vacations. So there were extra hours when he wasn't technically on duty but needed to be nearby. Hours to play basketball with Joe or chess with Michael. Hours to drive the girls to school. Hours to talk to them and be their friend. So many hours.

It was late when Frank stopped by the hospital. Thomas was sitting with Michael. The other siblings had gone back to the rented house they were sharing to get some rest. There was a wall up between Frank and the family now. Thomas was like a father lion, protecting his injured brother. But the wall came down just a little as they talked. Their eyes grew droopy and Thomas suggested a quick trip to the all-night cafeteria for some coffee. Michael had had another surgery to remove some damaged tissue from his left lung that afternoon, and Thomas was pretty sure he'd sleep through the night. The nurse's station was fairly close to his room. He would be fine for the short time it would take them to get some coffee.

****

Michael

Michael was startled awake by somebody roughly yanking one of the pillows out from under his broken right arm. The pillow was smacked down over his face and held there firmly. He struggled with all his strength, flailing his arms and legs, but the pillow wouldn't budge. He felt weaker and weaker, and just as the world started turning gray, he heard his nurse, Jackie, screaming. The hold on the pillow loosened. Michael managed to pull it off and saw a guy turning toward the frightened nurse. For the first time since the attack at Caroline's house, Michael felt wide awake.

"No," he thought. "Not this time. Not again." A huge surge of adrenalin kicked in, and he somehow managed to launch his broken body out of the hospital bed and clutch for the guy. Time stood still for a moment. The guy, Jackie, and Michael, were all surprised when his arms reached out and grabbed a piece of the guy's shirt as he crashed to the floor. The guy went down with him. Michael's IV pole tipped over with a crash. Jackie resumed her screaming and ran out the door. The guy smacked Michael hard on the arm to break his grasp. At this point an "accidental death" was obviously out of the question, and he could hear footsteps thundering down the hall. He quickly yanked out as many of Michael's tubes and wires as he could before picking up a chair, hitting Michael in the head with it, using it to break out the first-floor window, jumping out, and racing away.

Michael had managed to raise his arms, and the chair hit with a glancing blow. He hurt everywhere, but felt just a hint of satisfaction. He wasn't dead and neither was Jackie. He heard the people rushing into his room and lots of shouting voices.

Jackie was sobbing, "He just threw himself off the bed. I've never seen anything like it. He saved me."

Michael could hear sirens getting closer to the hospital. People were racing in and out of the door and bringing medical equipment. Tommy and Frank were standing over him. Frank looked down and said calmly, "You know, Bubba? This whole 'finding you on the floor covered in blood' thing is getting old. Could we maybe stop doing this?" Michael managed a crooked smile.

Accompanied by several police officers, Michael was whisked into a new room. Nurses and doctors hovered over him, stopping the bleeding, inserting a new IV line, bathing him, and getting him settled into a new bed. A portable x-ray machine was wheeled in so that they could get pictures of his head, chest, arms, and leg. His brand-new kneecap was dislocated, and his right arm re-broken, but other than that he didn't seem to have any new injuries. A decision was made to wait and see if his lung would work well enough that they wouldn't need to re-insert the chest tube. They also decided not to try and replace the drainage tube from his chest surgery. Michael was happy to be free of the tubes, but once the shock of what had happened wore off, he was in a great deal of pain. Medication was administered and he began to feel light-headed and sleepy.

****

The next morning, they decided that surgery was needed to repair his kneecap and to do some internal stitching where the chest tube had been so violently ripped out. Several hours later he was back in his room, once more heavily sedated. Thomas wondered how much more his brother's battered body could take.

Samantha Tierney and Carl Chase walked into the room followed by two men and one woman, all wearing suits. Their whole demeanor screamed "government employee." They showed badges to Thomas and then stated bluntly, "We're here to take Father Michael Wallace into protective custody. We have a plane waiting. We'll be moving him to a hospital in Washington DC today."

"What? No," said Thomas and Frank together. Frank looked at the two FBI agents who shrugged.

"Listen," said Thomas. "You can't take our brother away from us like this. Washington DC? No way. We need to be with him. This nightmare is only getting worse. And he's just come out of surgery. He can't be moved today."

One of the agents, who introduced herself as Agent Maria Gonzales dialed a number on her phone. "I have him right here, sir." She handed the phone to Thomas.

Thomas had met the President twice before, but never talked to him one-on-one. The President first gave his sincere condolences on the losses that the Wallace family had recently sustained. Then he spoke about how he needed to protect, at all costs, a witness to the murder of a United States Senator. And finally, he told Thomas that, as a friend of Senator Wallace, he was not about to let anything else happen to his son. A plane was standing by with all the necessary medical personnel and equipment to take Michael away. Thomas begged the President to find a way to protect Michael in Portland, where they already had rented a house and established a routine, or at least in North Carolina, where they could be close to home. He relented, and it was decided that they would move Michael to a hospital in North Carolina that very day with round the clock armed guards. Michael was going home.

CHAPTER TWENTY-TWO

MOVING

As gently as possible they dressed him in some sweat pants and a t-shirt and sweater from Joe's suitcase. His IVs were capped off and taped to his arms. They'd forgotten shoes and socks, but he wouldn't be doing any walking, so it really didn't matter. The media had heard about the latest attack and a few of them were gathered outside the hospital in hopes of gleaning any small fact in the ongoing attacks on Senator Wallace's family that would make their air time interesting. Their persistence paid off and those who were lucky enough to have brought cameras shot video as Michael was wheeled out on a gurney surrounded by police guards. He looked around groggily as they passed through the small crowd.

"Where are you taking Father Wallace?"

"Was anybody else hurt in last night's attack?"

"Were the Senator's murderers trying to silence him?"

"Can he identify them?"

"Have you caught the guys?"

"Father Wallace, how are you feeling?"

"Father Wallace, did you see who attacked you last night?"

"Dr. Wallace, is your brother alright?"

"Can he talk?"

And on and on and on. Thomas leaned over and whispered, "Just ignore them." But Michael seemed oblivious to his surroundings. When they got to the waiting ambulance, the agents lifted the gurney into the back. Thomas and the others had been informed that they would not be allowed on the government plane, and after heated arguments they'd had to accept that fact. Lisa was in the hospital room making phone calls and hastily organizing their trip back to North Carolina. Joe and Kelly were at the rental house packing and tying up loose ends there. As the ambulance pulled away, Thomas turned to the news people.

"I have a brief statement, and I won't be taking any questions. First of all, I'd like to thank everyone for the concern and care they've shown for my brothers and sisters and me, and my brother-in-law Matt and my nephew Paul during this horrible nightmare. The people of Portland, many of them strangers, have gone out of their way to help us. In particular, I'd like to thank the parishioners of St. Monica's Church. My late sister Caroline, her husband Matt, and their children were members there, and the parishioners have been more than generous and kind to us. We'd all like to thank them for their prayers. My brother, Father Michael, has received hundreds of cards and gifts, and appreciates them all. When he is able, he'll read each and every card. Please don't send any more gifts. We are overwhelmed by your generosity, but really can't accept anything more. We are going home to North Carolina, where Father Michael will continue to recuperate. We ask that you give our family time to heal and grieve."

"Dr. Wallace, why didn't you go with him?"

"Were those FBI agents?"

"Is he still in danger?"

"Is he in custody?"

"Do you think these killers were trying to punish your father and his family for his politics?"

"Have the police got any leads on the attackers?"

"Are you worried about the rest of your family?"

Thomas turned and walked back into the hospital.

****

Michael

"Where am I?"

"You're on a plane. My name is John Hill, and I'm going to be the doctor taking care of you now. We're on our way to North Carolina. They told you we were taking you there, right?"

"I guess. It's all kind of foggy."

"We'll be landing soon. How is your pain? Do you need any medication?"

"No, thank you. I really want to wake up."

Until last night Michael's guilt over surviving and not being able to save his family had been crippling him. But something about the last attack, and his struggle to save the nurse from harm, had awakened a will to survive in him. He wanted to be alert. He wanted to find out what had happened to his family and why. He wanted to remember. He'd gotten to the house too late to do anything for his parents and the children, and had failed Caroline in the last minutes of her life, but maybe he could help find the criminals who had ended it. The problem was that he was telling the truth about not being able to identify the third guy. He closed his eyes and tried to concentrate. He could not see the man at all. Wasn't that impossible? That agent had been right. He was literally lying under the man's foot as it crashed down on his chest, breaking ribs and collapsing his lung. Surely he had looked up into that man's face. Why couldn't he see him? Why couldn't he remember?

****

Samantha Tierney and Carl Chase went over the files for what seemed like the millionth time. To some extent they had to trust that agents who had been following the leads were doing a good job. The did flag any small thing that looked the least bit suspicious to check out themselves. They'd spent innumerable hours on the phone with other agencies. Every single clue was a dead end.

"Soooooo," said Carl. "The family?"

They had, of course, been checking into the family and friends all along. They couldn't find anything suspicious there, either.

"Michael?" he continued. "Pushed to the brink trying to please the old man and finally snapping? I know he was injured seriously. But why doesn't he help us more? Maybe he wanted it over for all of them. Murder and suicide by hire?"

"I don't know, Carl. I'm no psychiatrist, but it seems like that kind of crazy would have shown up in other ways. Somebody someplace would have noticed something off with him. Something big, not like changing his shirt all the time. I'm kind of with Frank Malone on this one. The old man was a terror, but they all seemed to genuinely love him, as well as their mom and sister. And killing kids takes a special kind of crazy. We can't rule any of them out, but it's unlikely."

"And the mysterious third guy?"

"I think Father Michael honestly thinks there was a third guy. Whether there was or not remains to be seen. He doesn't have one scrap of memory about the guy. Just that he exists."

"Money?" asked Carl.

"Yeah. The big motive. The agency got a copy of the Senator's will yesterday. He was loaded. But here's the thing. So are the kids. I mean, I guess more is always better. They're each getting about 20 mil. The grandkids all have trust funds that will put them through college and set them up nicely. Which brings us back to Father Michael. He gets 30 mil. and the ocean front house and all its furnishings. I don't know why he gets more. Maybe because he makes peanuts right now? What does a priest make? 30 or 40K a year? Still, I don't know what a priest is gonna do with all that money. From all accounts he's not worldly at all. But people have been wrong about their loved ones before."

What about Caroline's share? She died at the same time as her dad."

"That's a little unclear, but our lawyers think it will go to her husband. Little Paul is taken care of. The Wallace kids aren't going to fight over that much money. It'd be 4 mil apiece when divided among the five of them. Chump change for a Wallace. Besides, judging from what they've said in the interviews they seem genuinely fond of Matt Carter."

"Anybody in trouble? Gambling debts? Drugs? Girlfriends or boyfriends?"

"Not that we've been able to find. Apparently they are all saints. And they've all got alibis, although if any of them was involved it'd certainly be murder for hire. People like that don't like to get their hands dirty. I don't know. Where are you gonna find guys to hire who would cut a 3-year-old's throat, Carl?"

"I guess it depends on what you're offering."

"The all-American family. Not one skeleton in any of their closets. That seems just a bit off.

CHAPTER TWENTY-THREE

FUNERAL

The funeral for Caroline and the children had been heartbreaking. Michael was not well enough to attend, but the other four Wallace siblings were there with Matt and Paul and the Carter relatives. Various members of the Wallace family had flown to Portland, and St. Monica's church was packed. News vans surrounded the church, but the media was not allowed inside. Cameras rolled, however, when the hearses pulled up and one large casket was carried inside followed by two small ones. Madison Carter was being buried in her mother's arms. Professor Matthew Carter walked behind them in his dark suit, flanked by his parents, and carrying his surviving son who was sobbing against his shoulder.

The Memorial service for Senator and Mrs. Wallace had been delayed, but was finally going to be held at the Basilica Shrine of St. Mary in Wilmington. Security was heavy as many dignitaries, both political and religious had been invited. Once again news vans hovered outside the church, but this time some of the larger agencies had been given permission to film inside during the service. The President of the United States and his wife, many Senators and Congressmen, two Bishops and one Cardinal had been seen entering the church alongside numerous Wallace friends and family members.

As time for the service grew near four black limousines pulled up to the church, followed by cars holding policemen and bodyguards. No one wanted to risk another attack on the Wallace family. A man exited one of the cars, opened the trunk, and took out a wheelchair. This set the cameras whirring.

A female reporter speculated, "Does this mean that Father Michael Wallace is in one of those limos?"

It had been assumed, since Michael was still in the hospital, that he would be unable to attend the service. Over the last few weeks there had been a plethora of pictures of the other Wallace children, and of grandchildren, relatives and friends in the news. But there was only old footage of Father Michael Wallace, taken from talks he had given. The two short videos taken after the attack were unsatisfactory. One showed him on a stretcher being rushed out of his sister's house, and one on a gurney as he was taken back to North Carolina. You couldn't see him very well, and his condition was unclear. The family was being very protective of Father Michael, and the networks were beginning to wonder why. They were anxious to see how he was recovering and were, frankly, wondering about his mental and emotional well-being.

A bodyguard leaned into the car and effortlessly lifted Michael out and put him gently into the wheelchair. He was wearing his black clerical suit and sunglasses. He had on shoes for the first time since the attack. Other than bathing and putting on clean clothes, he had not been interested in his appearance and had declined his sister's suggestions. His dark curls were too long and he had grown a rather scruffy looking beard. The jagged scars on his cheek and forehead stood out against his pale skin.

Lisa wanted him to look good for the many cameras she knew would be trained on him. "My friend, Connie, would be glad to come to the hospital and cut your hair and help you shave." Then she added tentatively, "She could even put a little makeup on those scars."

"What? Makeup? No. I'm fine. And I'm keeping the beard."

"Well, ok. Forget about the makeup. What if she just trimmed the beard and cut your hair."

"No."

"Michael, it would make you look so handsome."

Michael rolled his eyes. "Yeah, Lees. That's the goal. To look handsome," he said sarcastically.

"Don't be so cranky, Mikey. I just want you to look nice. You know Mom loved it when you looked…"

"Cut the guilt trip, Lees. Just leave him alone," put in Joe, who rarely interfered. "He's an adult. He can decide how he wants to look."

The media people were restrained, but they kept their cameras trained on Michael as he waited patiently for his brothers and sisters and their families to exit the cars. When they were all assembled, they walked into church together, with bodyguards carrying Michael's chair up the steps.

Once inside Thomas pushed the wheelchair with Amy at his side. Joe walked next to Michael with his hand on his brother's shoulder. His wife Sara held his other hand. Behind them, Lisa walked with her husband, David, on one side and her brother-in-law, Matt Carter, on the other. Matt carried little Paul. Kelly and Stephen, and all of the other children followed. They made a tragic but poignant picture walking down the aisle in their somber clothing.

Matthew and Paul had flown to North Carolina earlier in the week for the Service. They were staying with Joe and Sara, and it seemed to be doing Paulie some good to be able to play with his cousins. The night of their arrival they'd all had dinner at David and Lisa's house and then gone to see Michael in the hospital. Paul climbed up on the bed with Michael and laid his head on his uncle's chest. He remained there for the entire visit.

There was a slideshow playing on a large screen at the front of the church. The family was about a quarter of the way down the aisle when a large picture of Michael and Caroline, taken at their last birthday, popped up. They were sitting together on the piano bench with arms casually thrown over each other's shoulders in the candid shot. Caroline was pointing at a smudge of cake on Michael's shirt and they were both grinning. It was the cake that had gotten on his shirt when Maddie hugged him. Little cake-face. Michael, reeling from the memory, involuntarily reached down and grabbed the wheels on his chair, causing it to stop and Thomas to stumble. Everyone froze. Joe leaned over and whispered, "Don't look at it." And then, "Michael, you have to let go of the wheels." Michael looked down at his hands, nodded, and let go of the wheels. They proceeded down the aisle to their seats. Michael, at his insistence, was lifted into a pew next to his sister, Lisa, instead of sitting in the pillow lined wheelchair. His sister helped him change from sunglasses to his regular glasses, as he was still having some amount of difficulty using his hands. He sat with his head down, not daring to look again at the slideshow. The formidable Mrs. Eleanor Murphy looked on from a middle pew with tears running down her face.

Mass was beautiful and poignant. Afterward several speakers talked of the wonderful life of service that Senator Wallace and his wife had led. Joseph Wallace, the son whom he never expected to amount to anything, beautifully eulogized his father. Kelly Wallace Thornton, that quiet ghost of a girl, beautifully eulogized her mother. Lisa glanced over and saw tears running down Michael's face. She put her arm around this man, her brother, her baby, and pulled his head down onto her shoulder.

And then a group of young children, dressed in choir robes, walked down the aisle. They were the choir from St. Joseph the Worker school where Michael had been assigned. Michael had often stopped by during their practices, and sometimes played the piano while they sang. He pulled himself together and sat up as the children sang. A rather unattractive young girl stepped up to the microphone and sang a beautiful solo piece. Michael smiled at them as they marched out of the church, some of them daring a little wave in his direction.

"The children really want to see you," said Lisa. "I know you're exhausted and hurting. Do you think you could manage a few minutes in the gathering room with them?"

"I'd like that," said Michael.

It was all he could do to remain sitting up, but Michael listened and smiled as the children chatted to him. A reporter and a camera man were allowed into the room for some pictures of Michael with the children. He hated the thought of being a story in the news, but agreed because he felt it might be good publicity for the choir and the school.

The camera man said, "How about a picture with one of the students standing next to Father?" He started to point out a beautiful little girl with blonde ringlets in the front.

"Yes," said Michael quickly. "How about Jenny?"

The homely soloist colored and hung back. The camera man looked annoyed, but nodded. Michael beckoned Jenny forward and motioned for her to bend down near him so he could whisper.

"Listen, Jenny. My sister told me this morning that I look pretty bad with these scars on my face and my messy hair. So I'll understand if you're embarrassed to have your picture taken with me."

Jenny's eyes grew wide. "Oh, no, Father! It's not that at all. You're very. You look. Um. But I think that photographer wanted Katie in the picture. She's really cute."

"Jenny, you have the best voice in the choir. You sang like an angel today for my family and me, and I want to have my picture taken with you. Someday when you grow up everyone will be asking for your autograph. And I'm going to save this picture of us from the news and have you sign it for me."

It turned out to be an amazing shot. The photographer saw the error of his ways when Jenny's brilliant smile lit up the picture with its joy.

Thomas stuck his head into the room. "Mikey, I'm sorry but we have to go now."

Corey, one of the students, gaped. "Can we call you Father Mikey?"

"Absolutely not," said Michael giving him a fake stern look.

A few minutes later Joe appeared. "I'm so sorry to cut your visit short, Bubba, but we really do need to go right now.

Corey looked at Michael with wide eyes.

"No," said Michael. "The first one of you to call me Father Bubba gets a week of detention."

As soon as they got Michael settled in the limo, Lisa gave him a pain pill and some water. He fell asleep on her shoulder on the way back to the hospital. The other siblings went on to the luncheon and explained to their disappointed family and friends that Michael would not be able to join them for lunch. They were not so foolish as to leave him alone again, though. His hospital room was heavily guarded.

CHAPTER TWENTY-FOUR

MORE QUESTIONS

While Lisa was away with her brothers and sister in Portland, David busied himself turning their first-floor den into a bedroom for Michael. The siblings had all wanted him to stay with them, but realized that David and Lisa's large beach home would probably be best. The den had its own bathroom and would be a perfect place for Mikey to recuperate. Lisa worked at home and would be there to care for him. The kids would be around to amuse him. It was a happy place. Or, at least it used to be. They hoped that it would be again someday.

Michael had been resistant to the idea.

"I don't want David giving up his den. I can go to a rehab facility. When I'm strong enough I can get an apartment and hire someone to help me. Or I can stay at Mom and Dad's with some helpers."

David laughed. "I have not used that den in forever. When I work at home it's almost always upstairs in our room where there are less distractions. And, Mikey. I really want you to be with us. We all do. The den is going to be your room, not just while you recuperate, but forever."

Both David and Lisa wanted him to consider their home as his own now, a place where he could come and relax or recharge on his days off after things got back to normal. If things got back to normal. They moved Michael into his new room after an uneventful two weeks at the North Carolina hospital. He still had round the clock protection, and his bodyguards stayed in the small guest house next to David and Lisa's home.

Physical and occupational therapists came to the house each day to help Michael recover his strength. He was not yet walking unassisted, but was able to use his damaged hands a bit more each day. He was awake more now and rarely took medication for pain. When therapy sessions were over, he spent his days swimming, napping, and reading. He did not write. He did not play the piano, even though the therapists kept encouraging him to do that as a way to exercise his hands.

****

Samantha and Carl felt that Michael might feel more relaxed if Frank Malone came along when they questioned him. They found Michael in his sister's family room. He was sitting in a recliner with a computer on his lap. He had shaved off the scraggly beard, and his hair looked damp from a shower. He was wearing shorts and a t-shirt and his glasses, and had a heavy looking brace on his right leg. There was a cup of coffee on the table at his side.

"Wow. Look at you, sitting up, wearing clothes, drinking coffee," said Frank.

Michael laughed. "The bar has been set pretty low for my life goals lately."

Lisa poked her head into the room. "Sorry to interrupt, but he needs to have some breakfast. Michael, do you want eggs or oatmeal?"

"I'm not really hungry."

"That's fascinating, Bubba. Do you want eggs or oatmeal?"

"I'll just have coffee, Lees."

She sighed. "Michael Joseph Wallace, your body is a temple of the Holy Spirit, and it's your job to take care of it. Right now, that means nourishing it so that, among other things, you'll stop looking like a war orphan. Now I don't care if you are hungry or not. Do you want eggs or oatmeal?"

Michael looked at the agents. "Any of you have sisters?" he asked with a laugh.

"Listen, Mikey," said Frank. "I wouldn't mess with her if I were you."

"Egg. Singular." He told his sister. "Please, Lees. Don't give me too much. It will just go to waste."

Lisa offered the agents coffee and breakfast. They accepted the coffee and made small talk for a bit. She brought a plate into the family room for Michael. "At least eat the egg, sweetie. And maybe a few bites of toast?"

He had been questioned numerous times by several different agencies, but try as he might he could not remember the third attacker. He was positive there was one, but had no idea what that person looked like. Today they wanted to, once again, take him minute-by-minute through what he had witnessed at Caroline's house.

"Father Michael, what was the first thing you saw when you opened the kitchen door?"

"I saw blood dripping down the refrigerator door. At first I didn't realize what it was. I thought somebody had spilled some kind of red sauce. But then I noticed it was on the walls and counter as well. And I realized it was blood."

"What did you see next?"

"Maddie." His voice faltered. The egg sat uneasily in his stomach, and he swallowed a few times trying to keep it down.

"Your 3-year-old niece, Madison?"

"Yes."

"And where was she, and what condition was she in?"

Michael closed his eyes. In his mind he chanted "Little cake-face. Little cake-face. Little cake-face." Aloud he said, "She was on the floor on the other side of the kitchen island. There was a gaping wound on her neck. She was covered in blood."

"And what did you do then?"

"I'm sorry. I'm going to..." he grabbed a napkin and pushed it against his mouth. Frank saw a nearby plastic lined wastebasket and handed it to him. Michael vomited into it. He closed his eyes.

"Michael? Can you go on?"

"Yes. Let's get this over with. After I saw Maddie I started running. I ran into the dining room." His voice faded out.

"And what did you see there?"

"My mom was lying on the floor. She was covering Anne with her body. Her arms were wrapped around Annie. I thought they were dead because they weren't moving and there was a lot of blood." He gagged.

"And then?"

"I heard my sister, Caroline, crying. And I ran into the family room."

It was there that his story always faltered. He could remember that his dad was lying on the floor. Dad had a huge gaping wound on his throat. His eyes were open and there still seemed to be life in them. Michael remembered wondering if he could see what was happening to his youngest daughter. He remembered two men leaning over Caroline with knives held high. He did not remember how he got on the floor. He did not remember seeing Matt or Paul. He did not remember what the third attacker looked like and only had a vague notion of the other two.

"Michael, if you could just remember one thing, anything, about that third guy it would be helpful. His voice. A piece of his clothing. Anything."

He shook his head sadly. "I know he was there. I know he was. I just can't remember."

They took him through it again and again and again, and Michael's eyes grew more haunted each time. He withdrew more into himself. Authorities had also been questioning Matt Carter, but his story remained the same. Paul was off limits to them. The family felt the questioning was doing too much harm to the 4-year-old.

CHAPTER TWENTY-FIVE

DR. GREEN

Dr. Deborah Green was a highly respected psychiatrist who had been a friend of the Wallace family for years. The siblings held a meeting and decided that the four of them should do some group counseling with Michael and their spouses included. Michael had not been included in the meeting and was not enthusiastic about the counseling sessions. But they began meeting twice a week in Lisa's family room.

Dr. Green artfully and carefully led them in discussions about the trauma they'd been through. They tentatively began to share their feelings of loss, despair, hopelessness, anger, and fear. Even Kelly spoke of not being able to sleep and the anxiety attacks she was having. Michael sat quietly. If he was listening, he didn't show it. His facial expression did not change. Sometimes he closed his eyes. Sometimes he stared out the window.

It was Thomas who finally exploded. He was angry at the world right now, and had reached his breaking point.

"Damn it, Michael! I'm sorry for what you saw. I know you went through hell, and I realize our grief isn't the same as yours.

"Grief isn't a contest, Tommy. My grief isn't more valid than yours."

"Well then why do you sit here day after day not speaking and not taking advantage of these sessions? Do you know what it's doing to the rest of us to see you turning into a statue? For God's sake, look at your sisters' faces."

"Tommy, please don't," said Lisa sharply.

Michael blinked and remained silent.

Dr. Green spoke to him. "Would you do me one favor, Michael? Would you answer just one question? I promise I won't ask you anything else for the rest of the day."

Michael looked at her but didn't answer.

"Actually, it's not a question. I'd like you to finish a statement for me. And I already know the answer. In fact, I'll write it down on this paper. You finish the statement and you can tell me if I got it right."

She wrote something down on her paper.

"Here's the statement. "I wish my siblings would ____."

"No," said Michael quietly. "I won't finish that sentence."

Thomas, who had not been able to scale back his anger, scowled at him. "Answer it! We all want to know what you want from us."

Dr. Green got up and handed the paper to Michael. "Did I get it right?"

Michael looked first at the paper and then out the window. He nodded slightly.

"May I share it with them?"

He didn't answer.

"Michael, if you don't answer I'm going to assume that you are ok with me sharing what is on this paper."

Michael sat still.

She handed the paper to Thomas. He read aloud, "Treat me like an adult. What the hell, Mikey? When have we ever not treated you like an adult? You've been terribly injured. That's why we've tried to take care of you. It's not fair to call that treating you like a child. You know damn well you'd do the same for any of us."

Suddenly he turned to Dr. Green. "But wait a minute. You knew he felt this way? He's barely spoken a word to you. How could you possibly know that?"

Dr. Green looked at Thomas. "How did you decide to have me come here and conduct counseling sessions for your family?"

Thomas answered, "We had a family meeting."

Dr. Green asked gently, "And who was at that family meeting?"

Thomas said, "All of us." He looked at Michael. "I mean. Well..."

Michael looked at him. "Right, Tommy. I'm not part of 'all of us.' I never was."

Thomas was flabbergasted. "Of course you were. You are. You were sleeping when we met. It wasn't a planned meeting. It was just casual. You've been so sick. Mikey, but you've got to know that we respect you and value your opinion."

"Really?" asked Michael bitterly. "Was I sick and hurt when you met with Dad to discuss his will? Was I part of 'all of us' that day? Five of you were there, right? Even Caro. Just not me. You know. When you decided to split the inheritance unevenly. When you decided to give me more than anybody else. Because you obviously think I can't take care of myself. Strangers seek my advice and value my opinion, Tommy. But my own family doesn't. They never have."

Thomas went to kneel by Michael's chair. "Bubba, we do respect you. I am so sorry if I've not treated you that way. You're the smartest of us all, and we all know it. You were out of town when we had that meeting."

"Give me a break, Tommy. You couldn't have planned it for a different day or even told me about it?"

"Ok, fine. Here's the truth. You were never meant to find out about that meeting. It was Dad. He didn't want you there, but not because he didn't respect you. Quite the opposite. Dad knew you'd object. You were the only one who could ever stand up to him and win, and I think he was afraid of not getting his way. He knew money doesn't matter to you. But he wanted you to have more because we all have careers where we make plenty of money. He said he just didn't want you to do without in an emergency or when you grew older."

"I really don't see myself having an thirty million dollar emergency, Tommy."

"I know. But there's not a big difference between what he left you and what he left us. Dad had a lot of money. And he left money to our kids as well. So it all evens out in the end."

"Thirty million dollars is a ridiculous amount of money, T. Why did he have to do that? Why did he set me apart and make me different? I hate that."

"Dad said your life was on a higher plane. He really said that, I promise. And he wanted you to have the house. He felt it was still your home. We all have established homes. We don't care what you do with the money. Dad wanted you to have it. But he's gone now. Give it away if you want. It's your decision and we'll respect it. I'm so sorry, Mikey. I don't know what to say except that it won't happen again."

It was two days later, at the next session, that Michael finally broke down. He was sitting quietly, but seemed to be paying more attention. Dr. Green suddenly turned to him. "Michael," she said, "Share one thing about your sister, Caroline."

Michael reached for his walker and stood up. He began to limp across the room.

Thomas felt his anger flaring up again. He just couldn't seem to control it since the attack. He said roughly, "Don't leave, for crying out loud. Nobody's going to force you to share anything."

But Michael walked to the piano and sat down on the bench. He hadn't played since the attack, and his hands were sore and stiff. He stretched his fingers out a few times and then began to play. It was her song, Rachmaninoff's Rhapsody on a Theme of Paganini. Kelly flew to her feet, clenching her fists. Lisa gasped and both she and Sara both put their hands in front of their mouths. David put his arm around Lisa. Thomas and Stephen hung their heads, and Joe got tears in his eyes. Amy clutched a couch pillow to her chest. Dr. Green did not understand what was happening, but obviously they did, and this was a highly charged emotional moment for the family. She sat still and observed. Michael played the song to the end. When he finished, tears were streaming down several faces.

"You played it all the way through for her," said Lisa softly.

"Do you know what she said to me? Her last words?" asked Michael. "Dr. Green, imagine that you and your family are being attacked. You are desperately fighting off these evil men and suddenly your brother appears in the doorway. You didn't expect him to be there. What would you say to him?"

"I can't even imagine being in such a situation," Dr. Green said quietly. "I don't know."

"Sure you do," said Michael. "You'd say 'help me'. That's what anybody would say. You'd look at your brother and say 'help me, Mikey.' That's what you'd do if you thought your brother was strong and capable. That's what you'd do if you though you could depend on him."

"Now wait a minute, Michael," said Thomas. There is no way you could have fought off three men with knives and clubs. Nobody could have. You are strong and capable, and Caro knew that. But you are not Superman."

Dr. Green spoke gently. "That's not what he means, Tommy. He doesn't think he could have won the fight. He just wanted to know she counted on him." She looked at Michael. "What did she say to you?"

Michael still had his back to them all. "She said, 'Run.' She screamed it. 'Run, Mikey.' She told me with her last breath that she knew she couldn't depend on me." The piano sounded a harsh chord as he put his arms across the keys and rested his head on them. He didn't know when he'd felt so tired. Even breathing seemed like too much work.

Joe sat down on the bench next to Michael and rubbed his back. "Listen, Bubba. I don't know a lot, but I do know this. Caro loved you with all her heart every day of her life. I don't know why she said that. But you were definitely her hero, and everybody knew it."

Dr. Green spoke again softly. "Michael, when you walked into that nightmare and saw your sister, what was the one thing you wanted more than anything in the world?"

Michael just shook his head.

"You wanted to save her, of course. You would have died to save her. But, Michael, when she saw you unexpectedly appear in that doorway, what do you think was the thing that she wanted more than anything in the world?"

He remained still.

"She wanted to save you, Michael. In that moment you wanted to save each other. It didn't have anything to do with who was or was not capable and strong. Saving you was more important to her than surviving. She just wanted to save you, in exactly the same way that you wanted to save her."

Michael sat up and turned around to face them all. "Black," he said. "His shoes were black. I could see them as he stomped on my chest. They were dress shoes."

CHAPTER TWENTY-SIX

FRIENDS

Michael was beginning to thrive. He would walk down to the ocean's edge, limping heavily, each morning with his breviary to pray. He began writing again. The others loved listening to him play the piano but Michael, ever the perfectionist, was disappointed in the length of time it was taking his abilities to return. His fingers were stiff and numb and wouldn't do what they'd done in the past.

His coworkers and a few friends had gotten the afternoon off to come for a visit. They'd only seen him from afar, at his parents' memorial service, and were looking forward to spending time together.

"Lees? Is it ok if I bake something?" he asked that morning.

"Mikey, you live here. You don't have to ask." Lisa was secretly thrilled to see him taking an interest in something that had previously given him joy.

"Well, but I don't know if you have the ingredients."

"If we don't have the ingredients, Mikey, I'd be happy to run to the store and get them."

He made an apple cake with caramel sauce to serve to his friends.

Michael needed to swim laps to exercise his leg, so several of the friends who had come to visit swam with him. Lisa had bathing suits of every size and often lent them out to company. After Michael finished his laps they tossed a ball back and forth and floated on pool chairs. Mrs. Murphy, Mrs. Whitton, a parish secretary, and Sister Joan, the school principal, had declined the offer to swim and sat with Lisa on the patio.

"You can go ahead and swim with them," Sister Joan told Lisa. We'll be fine sitting here chatting."

"I think I'll just let him spend some time with the guys," Lisa replied. "I can't tell you the joy it brings me to see him being able to relax a bit with his friends."

The gate opened and Thomas's wife, Amy came out onto the patio. Introductions were made all around and she joined the women.

"Hey, Mikey," she said. Do you want me to bring cheese potatoes or Mexican corn to your picnic tonight?

Michael stuck out his lower lip. "Do I have to choose?" he said in a wheedling voice.

"Fine," laughed Amy. "I'll bring both, you big spoiled baby. But you'd better eat them if I go to the trouble of making them."

Michael's friend, Father Kent, said, "Wow. Way to manipulate."

Michael laughed. "She always makes both. She'd be devastated if I chose one or the other."

"I heard that, Michael Joseph," said Amy with a mock severity in her voice. She and Thomas had started dating when Michael was 5 years-old. He was the ring bearer at their wedding.

"Listen," said Michael. "Both of those things are delicious, and that is the honest truth."

They had lunch then. Michael could hardly keep his eyes open as he ate.

Lisa turned to the group. "While Michael naps we could take a walk on the beach. Or you're welcome to take one of the boats for a ride. If you're not comfortable driving it, I'll be happy to come along."

"What are you talking about," asked Michael. "I'm not deserting my guests and taking a nap."

"No nap, no picnic on the beach tonight," Lisa told him.

"Lees. I'm not three years old."

"I'm sorry, Bubba. But seriously, you are exhausted. Your body is not going to let you stay awake now and still have the energy to enjoy the picnic later," she said.

"We're fine, Michael, really," said Kent. You go ahead and rest. We'll have lots of time to visit later.

Michael was exhausted, and secretly glad that Lisa was insisting.

Later that evening, he limped, with the large brace on his leg, down to the ocean where they had the picnic dinner. His siblings had made all of his favorite dishes, just as they'd done for the beach birthday parties.

Michael deeply appreciated their efforts and felt guilty for not being able to eat more. He called his nephew, George, over. "Hey, Georgie," he said quietly. Do you want this drumstick?"

George answered loudly, "My mom said I'm not supposed to let you trick me into eating your food."

Everyone laughed while Michael grumbled, "Well isn't your mom just right on top of things."

"Oh my gosh, Bubba," Lisa said when they finished. "I forgot to bring down your cake." She turned to his friends. "Michael is the best baker. You're going to love this cake."

"Lees," said Michael nervously as he saw Eleanor Murphy's eyes narrow. "It's not a big deal. Don't exaggerate."

"It's true, though, Mikey." She smiled at Mrs. Murphy. "Michael has been cooking and baking ever since he was a little boy and had to stand on a stool in the kitchen. You should taste his chicken salad."

Mrs. Murphy gave Michael a stern look. "Father. You've been lying to me." She looked a little hurt. "Have you been laughing about this behind my back."

Michael colored. "Oh no, Mrs. Murphy. I haven't done that at all. And I haven't said a word about our cooking sessions to anyone."

Mrs. Murphy softened. "Why did you do that, Father Michael?"

Michael looked down. "To tell the truth, I just wanted a friend. Rectories can be lonely places with everyone so busy and in and out all the time. Will you forgive me?"

Eleanor Murphy, who had been enchanted by Michael since day she met him, said. "We'll see about that. When you come home if, and that's a big if, I let you in my kitchen you're going to be expected to leave it spotless."

"Mrs. Murphy," said Michael laughing. "When have I ever left a mess?"

CHAPTER TWENTY-SEVEN

THEORY

This time Michael was working with his physical therapist, exercising his knee, when Samantha, Carl, and Frank arrived.

"I want him to swim some laps to cool down," said Ted, the therapist. "Are you guys in a hurry?"

They were not. Lisa brought lemonade and cookies out onto the patio.

Michael said, "Watch this, Frank." And, grinning, proceeded to walk with a heavy limp, but without his brace, out to the heated pool. He took off his sweatshirt, dove in, and began his laps. He was very thin and his chest and arms were badly scarred, but he looked healthier than Samantha and Carl had ever seen him. They chatted with Lisa until Michael finished his laps, pulled himself out of the pool, toweled off, and put his shirt back on. Lisa handed him a container of yogurt.

"Eat," she commanded.

"I'm not really..." he began.

"Hungry. I know," said Lisa. "You never are. Don't make me give you the speech. Eat the yogurt."

Michael raised his eyebrows. "You know, Lisa? Many adults get to decide when they are hungry and eat accordingly."

"Michael Joseph? Have I ever told you that you're my most annoying brother?"

"You have, Lisa Catherine. And it makes me so happy to know that I am number one in your heart."

Lisa rolled her eyes. "Stop stalling and eat the yogurt. And then have a cookie."

He did, and then they got down to business. Samantha and Carl and Frank started at the beginning and took him over the whole attack again step by step. The blood, Maddie, Mom and Annie, Dad, and then, "And then what happened, Father Michael?"

"It's ok to call me Michael. It seems like we've known each other forever."

"Thanks. Do you remember what happened after you got to the family room and saw your sister? Anything new?"

"I was hurting over something Caroline said to me that night. I think that might have played a part in my memory stalling at this point of the story. She told me to run. I took it to mean that she knew she couldn't depend on me, and that hurt. Dr. Green has shown me that it might have a different interpretation. I'm still trying to work out how I feel about that. But at any rate, she told me to run. Then suddenly I was on the floor and my knee was on fire. I guess somebody must have hit me with one of the pipes they were carrying."

"Do you know which of the men hit you?"

"Well, I'm not sure. But two of them were bent over Caroline, so it must have been the third guy. "

"And have you remembered anything more about him?"

Michael shook his head. "Just the shoes. But listen. Those shoes are a very vivid memory. I'm 100% sure that I'm right about them. Black dress shoes. And if I remembered those then there must be more in my head, right? I'm sure I'll remember more soon. I have to."

"Michael, do you know many of your dad's friends? Co-workers? Acquaintances? Has anyone contacted you in the last year about your dad? Complained about him?"

"You think I know the third guy, and that's why I can't remember. You think I don't want to remember."

"Not that you don't want to. But it's definitely in the realm of possibility that the trauma isn't letting you face the fact that you know him."

Michael thought for a moment. "I'm sorry. I want to help. I've been wracking my brain, thinking about this non-stop. I'm trying to remember everything, any small detail that could help."

"And have you come up with anything at all that you'd like to share with us?"

"Yes, but," He paused. "It isn't a fact. It's a theory. A feeling."

"And what is that?" asked Samantha.

"This whole thing wasn't," he hesitated. "It wasn't about dad at all. It was about us. Caroline and me."

"Oh Mikey, no," gasped Lisa.

Michael continued. "I can't think of a reason why someone would hate us so much. I just know that it was about us. It had to be."

Frank asked gently, "Why do you think that, Mikey?"

Michael looked at him. "You don't seem surprised. You think that, too, don't you."

Frank insisted, "Tell us why you think that."

"The others," started Michael, "Well, they were killed quickly. Within seconds. Their throats were slit, almost as if the attackers were just trying to get them out of the way. They didn't do that with Caro and me. It seemed that they wanted us alive. They wanted us to suffer. More than that, they wanted us to see each other suffer, inflicting painful injuries that wouldn't kill us and then waiting for the other one of us to see. I'm sure you guys have already noticed that. But it doesn't make any sense. Who hates us that much? Maybe I offended somebody in one of my talks, but how would that involve Caro? Maybe Caro and I did something that hurt someone years ago, in high school or even before. You see things like that happen on true life crime shows – someone holds a grudge for years and then acts on it. I can't remember anything like that, though, and I've really tried. I don't know the why. But if I caused this to happen to my family, well, I don't know how I'm going to live with that."

Carl asked, "How do you reconcile this theory with the fact that you weren't supposed to be there? You weren't due back at the house for a couple of hours."

Michael thought about that. "I don't know. Maybe they didn't realize that I had stayed behind at the church when the family came home. Maybe they'd have kept Caro alive that long. Maybe they'd have been satisfied if I just saw what she suffered. But it was us. Both of us."

****

"Should we tell him?"

"Absolutely not. He needs to arrive at it himself. Otherwise his testimony will be suspect. And we are going to get this guy."

CHAPTER TWENTY-EIGHT

ANSWERS

Michael was an early riser. Each morning when the children came down for breakfast, he'd be sitting at the kitchen table or in the comfortable family room recliner that David had bought for him.

"Where's Uncle Mikey," said George one morning. "I want to show him a picture I drew before I go to school."

"I guess he's sleeping in today, Georgie," said Lisa. "Let's let him rest. Maybe he had a bad night."

But when she got back from taking the kids to school Michael still had not come out of his room. Lisa waited until almost 10:00 and then began to get a little concerned. She hadn't known Michael to ever sleep this late. She knocked softly on his door and, getting no response, opened it and went in. Michael was sleeping on his back with his right arm thrown over his eyes. The wounds on his forearms and hands still shocked her every time she saw them. She felt so lucky that he was alive. But today his breathing seemed labored. Lisa sat on the bed and gently touched his shoulder. It was hard not to startle him these days.

"Bubba? Are you ok? It's almost 10."

Michael moaned and blinked his eyes open. He mumbled, "I feel sick, Lees. Hot and achy" and began trembling. She felt his forehead. He was burning up. She jumped up and went for a thermometer. His temperature was 104 degrees. She called Thomas at work.

"Give him some aspirin, and put a damp cool cloth on his forehead. I'll be there in 20 minutes," he said. But Michael turned his head away and she couldn't get him to swallow the aspirin.

When Thomas got there the thermometer read 105.5. "Come on, Mikey," he said. "Let's take a ride to the E.R." He tried to help his brother to sit up. Michael moaned and curled up in a fetal position.

"Soak a bath towel in really cold water. Don't wring it out all the way." he told Lisa. He went to the kitchen and filled a plastic bag with ice. Then he found two spoons which he used to crush up 4 aspirin and got a glass of water. He returned to the bedroom, added a small amount of water to the spoon, held Michael's head still and forced the mixture into his brother's mouth. Michael coughed and gagged. They stripped off his shirt and covered him with the cold towel. They put the bag of ice under his neck.

"Cold," gasped Michael, trying to move away from the ice and the towel.

"I know it is. I'm so sorry, Mikey," Thomas replied. Then he dialed 911.

The pneumonia wasn't surprising when you considered all the damage that had been done to Michael's lungs, but it was dangerous. They kept him on a bed of circulating cool air which made him shiver with the cold, but his fever raged on through the night. He became delirious and began to mutter and cry. Much of what he said was incomprehensible.

All four siblings remained at his bedside throughout the night, just as they had during those first few horrible days in Portland. Were they going to lose him now after he'd been doing so well? The thought was unbearable.

"No. Stop," he mumbled. "Caro!"

Kelly got a damp cloth and wiped his sweaty brow.

"He said. He said," moaned Michael. "He."

"Who, sweetie? What did he say?"

The words were slurred, repetitive, and hard to understand. "He said 'Oh, look.' He. He said 'P-p-prince Charming.' He said 'Got. Got here.' He said. 'Time. In time. Time to die. Time.'" Michael's head moved restlessly back and forth on the pillow. "He. He said, 'Watch. Watch him.' He said 'Die.' He. He said. 'Watch bitch.'" He moaned, "Don't hurt her. Stop!"

"Who, Mikey? Who said all that?"

Four Wallace children felt their hearts break into pieces when Michael said clearly, "Matt. He said, 'Watch.'"

****

Paul sat in a room with the child psychiatrist and Frank Malone. The courts had mandated this session, and Matt, his parents, Samantha Tierney, and Carl Chase were on the other side of the two-way mirror. They'd brought Frank along for the questioning as they felt he'd built up a rapport with the child. Paul, Frank, and the psychiatrist were playing a game of Chutes and Ladders.

"Hey, Paulie," said Frank. "Remember when we were talking about those bad guys who came to your house?"

The little boy looked up hopefully. "Did you catch them, Frank?"

"Not yet, Paul. But we're trying awfully hard. Can you answer some more questions to help me catch them?"

"You get to climb the ladder, Frank. You landed on red."

"Oh, cool. Thanks buddy," said Frank, moving his game piece. "Paul? Do you remember waking up in the family room with your arm hurting? Maybe we could tell Dr. Kelly about that, and he could help us try and figure out a way to find the bad guys."

"Is Dr. Kelly a cop?"

"No. But he's really good at figuring things out," said Frank. "So, I forgot what you said about waking up in the family room. Was your head hurting when you woke up?"

"My arm was hurting," said Paul. "Not my head."

"Oh, that's right. Who did you see in the family room? Do you remember?"

"I saw my mommy and my daddy and grandpa and Uncle Mikey. And I saw the bad guys."

"And how many bad guys were there?"

"Two. Two bad guys."

"And what was everybody doing?"

In the waiting room, Samantha saw Matt unconsciously clench his fists.

"Grandpa was sleeping on the floor, I think. He had a sore on his neck. Uncle Mikey was on the floor, too, but he wasn't sleeping. His hands were all red. Like when you finger paint with red paint. He was trying to grab one of the bad guys around the legs because the bad guys were hurting Mommy. She was fighting and crying."

"Good job remembering, Paul," said Frank. "Oh, look. Now it's your turn to climb a ladder."

Paul grinned and moved his piece. "I'm gonna win. I'm the closest."

"Paulie?" asked Frank, almost holding his breath. "What about your daddy? What was he doing?"

"Daddy?" Paul frowned at the game.

"Yes. Daddy. Was he sleeping, too, like grandpa?"

"No. He was standing up. He was helping Uncle Mikey fight the bad guys."

Frank was confused. "How was your daddy helping Uncle Mikey?"

"With his foot. Daddy was pushing him with his foot. I think so Uncle Mikey could get closer and reach the bad guys better."

****

The chair tipped over as Thomas flew to his feet. "I'm going to kill him. I'm going to fly out there and slice him to ribbons. And then I'm going to bring him back to life so I can kill him again."

"Shh. Tommy! Look what we have in this bed right here in front of us. Don't scare him. Don't wake him," begged Lisa.

Joe said, "Wait. Tommy. Think. Michael is delirious. He's medicated. He has a high fever."

"It's the truth, Joe. I know it is. You know it is. He couldn't make that up in his condition. And you know Matt used to try and get under Mikey's skin by calling him Prince Charming. It all makes sense."

"I know," said Joe. "I believe him. I'm sure it's true. But think. We can't do anything to jeopardize Matt getting arrested and punished. I know you want to kill him. We all do. But that is not who we are. It's not who Mikey is. We have to be smart about this, Tommy. And we can't talk to Michael about this either."

"What? Why not?"

"Because he has to remember by himself. He has to remember when he's not delirious, when he's not feverish. He's going to be a witness someday, Tommy, and we can't influence him in any way. There is little to no physical evidence. Mikey is the only witness, except for a 4-year-old child. At this point a good defense attorney could tear Michael apart. We have to let him get stronger and more confident in his memories. Matt could get away with this if we aren't careful, and Michael could be destroyed."

"Joe. What if the fever breaks and he doesn't remember? How can we possibly pretend to him that we don't know? And what about Matt? What if he calls? How could we talk to him without going insane?"

"We have to. For Mom and Dad. For Caro and those beautiful children. Even for Gerry Pelton, who lost his life trying to protect them. We have to, Tommy."

****

The chair tipped over as Matt flew to his feet. "He's wrong. I was unconscious. He's just a baby. He's traumatized and doesn't remember."

Matt's parents looked stunned and confused. Carl Chase looked at him coolly and said, "Calm down, Professor Carter. We'd be glad to have you tell us again what you remember. There are several things about this attack that are confusing to us. You say you were unconscious. You say you didn't see your brother-in-law at the house. You and Paul both say there were two attackers. Father Michael says there were three. He was obviously there at some point, when he got so seriously injured. Your son says he saw his uncle. He says you were standing up when he slipped out of the house. Do you want to change your statement? Maybe you could take a lie detector test to clear this up once and for all."

"You're trying to trick my son and railroad me because you can't find the real attackers," said Matt heatedly. "Leave my son alone, and go do your job. He's a baby. The government is pressuring you because my father-in-law was a Senator, so you're grasping at straws. Paul and I both saw two guys because that's how many guys there were. Michael doesn't know what he's talking about. He got bashed on the head, and if you really knew him, you'd realize that he's kind of a weirdo anyway. I'll bet Frank here could tell you some stories. I'll bet he's seen some things. Mikey – why they call a grown man Mikey is beyond me – is a bundle of nerves. Obsessive/compulsive. Ask him how often he changes his shirt. He's a nut case. I certainly wouldn't put any stock in anything he says even if he hadn't gotten his skull cracked. Ask his brothers and sisters why they have family meetings behind his back. Ask them that. My wife was there and all the rest of them. But not holier-than-thou Michael." He seemed to suddenly realize he was ranting and pulled himself together. "None of us is talking to you again without an attorney present."

CHAPTER TWENTY-NINE

BIRTHDAY

Michael arrived at the beach the week of his 29th birthday in high spirits. He had the whole following week off, and better yet Caroline and Matt and their four kids were spending some time at Mom and Dad's house as well. He talked to his sister on the phone often, but hadn't actually seen her or her family in quite some time. He dropped off his bags in the bedroom that had been his for his entire life, changed into casual clothes, and wandered down to David and Lisa's house. Caroline flung herself into his arms as he stepped through the door.

"Wow. Look at you," said Michael as he took in her shorter sleek hairstyle, make-up, jewelry, and stylish clothes.

"Do you like it?", she asked.

"Come on, C. I'd like you in a paper bag with a shaved head."

"But... really. Do you like it?", she asked again.

Michael had never known Caroline to give a whit about her looks or what anybody thought of them. This new, tentative Caro confused him.

"Of course, Caro. You look lovely," he answered.

A bit of the old Caroline surfaced and she snorted, "Lovely? Gimme a break, Bubba."

"Where are the guys?" Michael asked as he headed for the kitchen to get a beer.

"Beer run. Sorry," said Lisa. "There's soda here, though."

The three of them grabbed a soda and went out to sit by the pool and chat. Things grew animated as they reminisced about the time Caroline had accidentally kneed him in the groin, causing the hilarious conversation between Michael and his prim and proper mother.

"By the way, I never paid you back for that," said Michael. And he jumped up, scooped her into his arms, and unceremoniously dumped her into the pool.

Caroline surfaced laughing and screaming. "You've had it now, mister. You are so going into this pool." She swam toward him purposefully.

Michael dove in fully clothed. He surfaced and laughed. "Your move, Miss Caroline." Giggling, she jumped on his back and dunked him, and they splashed around trading threats and laughing for several minutes. It felt so good to be together. Michael was once again glad they would have the whole week to visit. The Bishop had suggested that he earn a doctorate, and between studying, speaking engagements, parish work, and writing, he'd been working really hard lately, often long into the night. He was exhausted and hadn't felt this carefree in a long time.

Suddenly Caroline's smile faded. "Oh, damn. My hair." She pulled herself out of the pool and toweled off, natural curls springing up all around her head. "I've got to go change and fix it again. Michael, what is wrong with you?" she said, suddenly angry. "You need to stop throwing me in the pool. It's childish. We're way too old for that nonsense."

Michael was shocked. They had been throwing each other into the pool since they were children, and Caroline was the biggest offender. He couldn't remember a birthday when one of them hadn't pushed the other in. She'd always laughed and thought it was uproariously funny in the past. Never once had it annoyed her.

Michael stammered, "I. I'm sorry, C. I…"

Water was streaming off her shining curls. Most of her make-up had come off in the pool and a bit of mascara ran down her face. To him, she had never looked more beautiful.

"And look at you. You're in the pool with your shoes on. It's time to grow up, Michael."

She turned and stormed away.

He got out of the pool dejectedly and turned to Lisa.

"Look at her, Lees. She's so beautiful. Why is she smoothing down her hair and wearing all that makeup? Why can't she relax and have fun? I don't get it. She's never been upset about being thrown in the pool before. Do you think she's really mad at me?"

Lisa threw him a towel. "Oh, honey. Women and their hair. She's not mad at you, just frustrated. Curls are hard to tame."

"I don't understand why she has to tame them all of a sudden," he grumbled.

"Of course you don't understand. You're a man. And, to be honest, even most men care at least a little bit about their looks. I say this with abundant love, Mikey, but you are an odd duck.

"I'm aware of that. And I care about my looks. They bring me nothing but trouble. But the point is that she never used to care. Why all of a sudden?"

"Why don't you ask her?"

"I can't. Things have changed between us."

"Things haven't changed. Give her some time. Take a walk on the beach together. Talk to her."

"Maybe." He sounded doubtful.

Lisa sighed. "Listen, Bubba. Women go through phases. Give her time to cool down. You have some clothes in the top dresser drawer in the guest room if you don't want to go back to Mom and Dad's to change."

Michael stopped by the door to remove his shoes and set them off to the side of the patio to dry. He heard Matt's sharp voice. "Damn it, Caroline. Can't you act like an adult woman for even one night? Just when I thought you were looking nice and I could feel proud of you at this party, you have to pull this crap. Your parents' friends will be here, and look at you. The minute you get anywhere near your brother you turn into a hellion."

"I'm sorry, Matt," said a voice that did not sound at all like his sister. "It was an accident."

"Accident, my ass. Your brother threw you in the pool."

"No, Matt. It wasn't like that. I wasn't watching where I was walking, and I tripped over a shoe and fell into the pool. I'll just go down to Mom and Dad's and change. And it won't take long for me to fix my hair. It won't happen again. I promise."

Michael waited until his sister had gone out the side door before entering the house.

"Well, if it isn't Prince Charming," sneered Matt. "Swimming with the Princess?"

"Uh, no," lied Michael. "After Caro fell in, Lisa dared me to jump in as well to make her feel better. Excuse me. I'll just go and change."

Later Caroline reappeared, looking like a model. She wore a sundress and sandals with heels. Everyone else was barefoot and in shorts and t-shirts.

They had their usual potluck birthday dinner on the beach, and his mom and siblings had made all of his favorites. Michael hadn't had trouble with his stomach for a while and was starving. He decided to risk it and filled his plate.

Matt, walking behind him, commented. "Are you going to eat all that? Must be nice to just eat whatever you want and stay so thin. Some people have all the luck."

Michael shrugged. He started to answer but decided that a party wasn't the time to get into his digestive problems. And besides, he'd never liked to talk about personal issues.

They built a big bonfire later that evening and made s'mores. 3-year-old Paul insisted on roasting his own marshmallow over the bonfire. It promptly caught fire and burned until it was blackened. He started to cry. Michael, who had spent a considerable amount of time roasting a perfectly toasted brown marshmallow called him over.

"Hey, Paulie. That kind is my favorite. Will you trade with me, please?"

Paul looked at him suspiciously. "No it isn't. Nobody likes the burned ones."

"I do, though. Can I please have that one?"

Paul handed him the stick and Michael popped the burned marshmallow into his mouth and ate it.

"Delicious," he declared. "Thanks for trading. You take this one and make your s'more. And after you eat it will you make me another marshmallow just like that one, Bubba?"

Paul had stopped crying and now he giggled. "I'm not Bubba. You're Bubba."

Michael smiled at him. "Well, I guess we're both just a couple of Bubbas."

Paul took the stick with Michael's perfect marshmallow, and ran to his grandmother for a graham cracker and a chocolate bar.

"Me and Uncle Mikey are a couple of Bubbas," he told her proudly.

"Are you, now," said Catherine, smiling at her son over the happy toddler's head as she helped Paul make his s'more. "Well the world had better brace itself if there are two of you."

Matt had been drinking nonstop. From the chair next to Michael he said in a low voice, "Don't interfere with my son again. He needs to learn that everything in life isn't perfect for us, like it is for some people. He needs to learn that there are consequences to his actions."

Michael opened his mouth to say, "Come on, Matt. He's only three," but wisely decided against it and kept quiet.

Matt continued, "You waltz in and give them whatever they want. That's why all the kids flutter around you like you're the Pied Piper. You're never around to deal with their nonsense. It's not right that a child should prefer his uncle to his father."

Michael, shocked, replied, "He doesn't prefer me, Matt. You're wrong. Your kids adore you. They just don't see me that often, so I'm a novelty to them. I apologize. I didn't mean to interfere."

Matt scowled, "Mr. Perfect," he muttered under his breath.

Later the birthday cakes were brought out, chocolate for Caroline and lemon for Michael as usual. Michael had long ago given up having a piece of each and gratefully accepted the rather large piece of lemon cake that his mother handed him.

Paul wandered over. "What kind of cake are you eating, Uncle Mikey?"

Michael answered, "Lemon. It's my favorite."

Paul went running to his grandmother. "I want lemon cake, too. It's my favorite. Just like Uncle Mikey."

****

Whenever Michael was at home, he took a late-night walk on the beach with his mother, just the two of them. It was one of his favorite parts of the visit.

"Mom," he said tonight. "Do you think she's happy?"

His mother did not ask who he meant. "She's a grown woman, Michael. And she's always been independent. She can take care of herself."

"But can she? I feel like she's changed, especially in the last year. For the first time in my life I can't talk to her about things. She got really angry with me this afternoon and I don't understand why. And, Matt. I've always suspected he didn't care for me, and it seems to get worse as time goes by. I can't figure out how I've offended him. He seems downright hateful sometimes."

"So, is this about Caroline? Or about you?"

"Her," Michael sighed. "And me. I don't know. I really try to like Matt, but the way he talks to her makes me angry. And it always gets worse when he's been drinking. You don't think he's abusive, do you?"

"Michael," his mother said gently. "You and Caroline have always shared a heart. That's a hard thing for a spouse to deal with. And marriages go through seasons. Maybe this is a rough season for them. Dad and I... well, we've had our rough patches as well. Dad hasn't always been an easy man to live with. But I love him. I trust that Caroline loves Matt."

"And maybe," she added. "Maybe he's a little jealous of your relationship. Or just of you. Your life looks pretty easy to an outsider who doesn't understand your struggles. He only sees you on vacation with the people who love and admire you. He doesn't see how hard you work. That's a good reason, son, for you to stay out of it. But do keep trying with Matt, honey. Caroline must see something in him that you don't."

Michael spent a lot of the next week surrounded by family, but alone. He went for long solitary walks on the beach and sat on the sun porch writing. Some afternoons he sat in the Lucky Duck nursing a bourbon and talking to Charlie. He shooed the children away and told them he had work that had to be done. It disappointed them, and it hurt him to see this week with them that he'd so looked forward to slipping away. If he hadn't said Mass for them each morning and eaten dinner with them each evening it would have been a very sad vacation. Still, there was no more tension with Matt that week. And the new quieter and reserved Caroline seemed to be at peace.

She'd come out to the sun porch one day while he was writing.

"Mikey," she started. "I want to apologize…"

"It's ok, C," he said. "I'm sorry, too."

"No. You didn't do anything wrong. We've always tossed each other into the pool. I was just having a bad day. And that crack about growing up was cruel. You're certainly more mature than me. I wouldn't want you to ever change. I love you, Bubba, and I hate that I hurt you."

Michael ventured, "Are things…ok? With you? I mean, not this week. But at home. Are things ok? I feel like you're trying to change and I don't understand why. You're perfect the way you are."

Caroline laughed. "I am so far from perfect, you big goofball. Things are ok. Not great, but ok. We're working on it. Please don't worry about us, Mikey. Nobody's life is perfect all the time. We'll get through this and be stronger for it."

CHAPTER THIRTY

REMEMBERING

Michael

After two days on antibiotics, Michael's fever broke. He spent three more miserable days in the hospital getting oxygen and strong doses of medication that upset his touchy stomach. But the pneumonia had taken a toll on him. His physical condition had deteriorated considerably by the time he was ensconced back in his recliner in David and Lisa's family room. He was very weak and needed to use his walker again. Walking from his bed to the recliner winded him. He felt constantly cold, so they pulled out the lovely lap blanket that his sister-in-law, Sara, had made for him while he was hospitalized in Portland.

Michael was quiet and withdrawn again, but not disinterested. Still, no one dared to asked him about the things he'd said in the hospital. No one asked him if he'd had any dreams. And Michael did not volunteer any information. He wasn't hungry. He didn't want to read or watch movies. He didn't want to swim or play the piano. He prayed quietly in the house instead of going to his favorite spot on the beach. He stared out the window. A depressing pall fell over the house.

He asked for a private session with Dr. Green. They walked down to the beach. Michael had a great amount of difficulty as he was still very weak and hadn't exercised his leg lately, and at one point had to put his arm around Dr. Green's shoulder and lean on her. They sat in beach chairs, Michael wrapped in a blanket although the day was warm.

"I don't know where to begin," he said miserably. I don't know what to do."

"Just talk, Michael," encouraged Dr. Green. "We'll sort things out later. Begin anywhere. Just get it off your mind."

"It's the attack. I think I know. I think I remember. I think I know who did this to us." He looked sideways at her, but she remained still and calm and continued to listen.

"But I'm afraid. This memory came back when I was in the hospital with a high fever. I was having crazy dreams." He faltered. "Dr. Green. I dislike this person intensely. What if I'm making a mistake? What if I accuse somebody because of my personal feelings? I don't want to tell anybody about it because... what if I'm wrong?" And under his breath, "Please let me be wrong."

"Michael," said Dr. Green quietly. "On the day that you played Caroline's song for us on the piano you had a memory. Was that memory accurate? Are you sure of it?"

"The shoes," said Michael. "Yes. I'm sure. It's very clear."

"And do the shoes make sense and fit in with these new memories?"

Michael thought for a minute. "They do. I saw black dress shoes. And he was wearing black dress shoes that night. They were all dressed up for the Mission. He had on black pants. Black shoes. A sport coat and tie. It fits."

"Are you struggling because you think the memory is false? Or because of your guilt for disliking a person that Caroline may have loved?"

"You know," said Michael.

"I think you just inadvertently gave me a big clue. Or maybe not so inadvertently. I think you want, and more than that, need to talk about this. So think about it, Michael. Is the memory real? Does it make sense? Is there evidence? Only you can decide. But, Michael, people often discuss hunches and guesses with the police. Pointing them in a direction doesn't mean that you are accusing anyone. You can tell them you're not sure. It might be helpful to give them something more to investigate, though."

Michael laid his head against the back of the chair and closed his eyes. He listened to the waves for a few minutes, one of his favorite sounds. He could relax here, on this beach where he'd spent most of his life.

"Dr. Green," he said. "It was him. It was Matt. I think I've known all along. I didn't want to believe it. I don't understand it." He choked up. "His own kids. He did that to his babies. I can see him hating me enough, and maybe my parents. He must have loved Caro once, though. Don't you think? He must have loved her once. And those babies..."

Dr. Green leaned back in her own chair and closed her eyes. She reached over and took his hand and let him cry.

Michael wiped his eyes on his shirt. He turned to her and said, "Dr. Green, how am I going to tell the others? This is going to hurt them so much."

"Michael," she said gently. "They already know."

His face fell. "Of course they do. And they haven't said a word to me. Protecting the baby again."

"No, Michael," she insisted. "Not this time. They only found out because you said his name in the hospital. They didn't dare mention it to you. Don't you see? You had to remember on you own. Otherwise your testimony would be suspect. Now they can say that they never mentioned his name to you, and it will be the truth."

"Testimony," he breathed. And he closed his eyes again to listen to the ocean.

****

This time when Agent Tierney and Agent Chase came to question Michael, his Uncle Bill was there to represent him. The questioning was much more formal even though they were casually seated around the family room for Michael's comfort. His siblings were sitting in the kitchen talking quietly. There was no point in keeping them away at this point. They'd already heard everything Michael had to say, both when he was feverish and when he was well.

They took him through it. Now that his memory had kicked in, he was remembering small details that he hadn't mentioned before.

"I tripped over some boots in the mudroom before I went in."

"Boots? We didn't find any boots in the mudroom."

"I tripped over them and set them off to the side."

"What kind of boots?"

"Cowboy boots, I think."

A possible piece of evidence. Would Michael's DNA be on someone's boots? Some fiber from his clothes? Fingerprints? Blood from their socks transferred to the interior of the boots?

"I remember now that there was a knife in Maddie's chest. I think I've been blocking that out. The knife was huge." He swallowed. "She was so tiny and that knife was so big."

This new information matched what they had observed at the crime scene, and gave credence to his other memories. No knife had been found, but there had been a stab wound in the child's chest, in addition to her throat being cut. The killers had found the time to gather up and cart away their weapons.

"Michael, tell us about the family room. Every minute from the time you stepped into the doorway."

He took a deep breath and sighed heavily. "I stopped in the doorway. I think I was stunned. Dad was lying on the floor. His throat was cut and there was a lot of blood. His eyes were open. They didn't look glassy or anything, though. Just for a second an incredible sadness washed over me to think that the last thing he saw was his family being slaughtered. He had such great hopes for us all."

"And what else?"

"I don't remember seeing Paul. There were two guys bent over Caroline. She saw me and screamed at me to run. Maybe I should have done that. But I just froze. Maybe if I'd gotten away, I could have called someone. Maybe I could have..." He gulped again.

"Michael, your sister was beyond hope at that point. They all were. Actually, so were you."

"I guess. It's just so hard to think that there was something, anything I could have done if I hadn't frozen in that doorway. At any rate, suddenly I was on the floor, and I felt a huge pain in my knee. Matt was standing over me holding some sort of pipe or club. He said something about me getting home in time to die. He called me..."

"What did he call you?"

"It's kind of embarrassing. He called me Prince Charming. He used to do that to tease me. It was really more of an insult, but at the time I didn't think he realized that. He hit me across the face with the iron bar. Then He spoke to the two guys and told them to hurt me. They turned away from Caro and started jabbing at me with knives and hitting me with the bars. I put up my hands to try and defend myself and they kept stabbing my hands and arms and chest. They didn't try to cut my throat, though. Matt told them to stop. He told Caroline to look at me. He said something about me not being so perfect now. She was screaming. They went back to her with the knives." He shuddered.

"Can you go on?" asked Samantha softly.

"That's when Matt started stomping on my chest. Over and over again. I felt things breaking. I couldn't breathe. Matt told me to look at my sister. He said something about the perfect twins being damaged goods now. He laughed. Caro was moaning. After that all I remember is pain and hearing different voices. Somebody said, 'Oh, Mikey.' And then I don't remember anything until I woke up in the hospital."

"And Matt didn't have any injuries at all?"
"Not when I saw him."

CHAPTER THIRTY-ONE

MATT

He'd noticed her in class even before they got assigned to be in the same study group. Caroline Wallace. She wasn't really his type. He liked elegant, well-dressed, model types, who took time over their hair and make-up. And he could get them, too. Matt Carter was handsome, smart, and talked a good game. He was a good actor and could become whoever people wanted him to be.

Caroline was different from other girls. She was gorgeous, sure, and that was definitely a must for Matt. But she had a bohemian, devil-may-care kind of look. She didn't seem to try at all to tame her long dark wild curls. She wore little or no make-up and came to class in jeans and t-shirts. She had an easy, self-confident way about her that frightened him a little. He liked girls he could control. But she had something the other girls didn't have – a rich important senator for a father. And Matt Carter had decided at a very young age that he was going to go places in life, no matter the cost.

His dad was a mailman. A mailman, for crying out loud. When people asked Matt what his father did for a living, he said that his dad worked for the Post Office. It sounded better than mailman, but not much. His mom was a nurse. That was ok, although doctor would have been better. In high school everybody knew that he lived in a boring, average, slightly run-down house and had boring, average parents. But here, in a college far away from his home town, he could reinvent himself. So his dad "worked for the Post Office" and his mom worked "in the medical field". He was determined that he was going to marry this senator's daughter. This rich senator's daughter. This was going to be his ticket out of his embarrassing family. He was finally going to get the attention he deserved. Matt started playing a part. He took the classes she took. They studied together. He liked what she liked. He let her take charge. He showered her with attention.

They dated for two years, and he kept up his façade for the whole time. He was polite and solicitous, but not over the top. Caroline liked her friends a bit on the feisty side. He started going to Mass with her and volunteering at the homeless shelter with her. That was unpleasant, but he figured it would look good on a resume someday.

When things got more serious between them, he was invited to the family's ocean front house in North Carolina. Holy crap. That place was a mansion. Matt was an only child, but Caroline had five siblings. And she was a twin.

When they pulled up to the house there was an old Honda that had seen much better days in the driveway.

"Oh, Mikey's here," said Caroline excitedly.

"That's his car?" asked Matt. "I thought your dad gave you a car for graduation."

"Oh, he did. Michael didn't want one."

"What? Why not?"

"He asked if he could have a piano instead."

"But he can't take a piano to school with him."

"I know. He likes to play it at home, though. The one we used to have was kind of old and battered."

Matt tried to think of something nice to say about this very dumb decision. "Well, that's certainly unusual."

"Yeah. Mikey is an unusual guy. You're gonna love him."

Matt hated him. Michael looked just like Caroline with the same messy curly hair. His was kind of a medium length and kept falling over his forehead. Everyone seemed to flutter around him like he was the king of the world. The guy was studying to be a priest. What a loser. But everybody in the high and mighty Wallace family dropped everything to see to his every whim.

Matt got on well with the Senator, the only one who didn't cater to Michael's every need. And the Senator seemed to like him. He knew how to fit in. He dressed well and was respectful. He held his own in family volleyball games. He was helpful with the guy jobs around the house, like carrying chairs that needed to be moved and starting a charcoal fire and grilling. That weird Michael was often in the kitchen baking cookies with his sisters or sitting on the counter laughing with them or helping them fix dinner. What a wimp. The family called him Mikey, for Pete's sake, like he was some kind of giant baby. Still, Matt knew that Caroline wouldn't be very happy if he didn't get along with her twin. He tried to find some common ground so that he could fake it.

"Michael (he refused to call him Mikey), did you play any sports in school?"

Michael shrugged, "My dad always insisted we do at least one sport and one musical instrument."

"Yeah? Which sport did you play? You look like a tennis player."

"Do I? I played football and baseball."

"Huh. You're kind of... um... lanky for football aren't you?"

Michael smiled. "Are you trying to think of a polite way to tell me I'm skinny?"

It was just like that jerk to embarrass him. Matt didn't want the Wallaces to think he was putting down their superstar. He was seething inside but managed to sound repentant. "Oh, gosh no. I'm sorry. I just meant..."

"It's ok. I had a few more muscles back when I was playing." He laughed, "You know how they do those before and after pictures of guys who work out and get muscles? I did the after first. Now I'm the before."

"So, what position did you play in football?" Matt had been on his high school team as well, but didn't get put in that often. His coach had been a real idiot.

"Oh, I played a couple of different positions." He actually acted like he was disinterested or embarrassed instead of proud. He must not have been good at it. Not surprising, given what a pansy he seemed to be. Probably afraid of being tackled. What a wimp.

The Senator walked into the room. "False humility doesn't become you, Michael." To Matt he added, "He was the quarterback on his high school team for three years. They won the state championship in both his junior and senior years. He played his first year in college, as well." He gave Michael an exasperated look. "But then he quit because his interests were elsewhere."

You might know this asshole was a quarterback. "Quarterback, huh. I suppose your girlfriend was the head cheerleader."

"No," said Michael, clearly uncomfortable.

"No girlfriend, then?" He was probably gay. Wouldn't be surprising with all the time he spent cooking with his sisters and playing the piano and walking on the beach with his mom.

Catherine spoke up. "His girlfriend was on the volleyball team. A lovely girl. She was their highest scoring player. She set a school record, and played in college as well. Obviously they had to part ways when Michael decided he wanted to enter the seminary. That's her, in the photo on the mantle. You don't mind that I keep that photo up, do you, sweetie? I really did love Julie, and I hope she's doing well."

"It's fine, mom. Part of my past, I guess."

"Let's watch the video of that final game," said Caroline suddenly.

"What? No," sputtered Michael.

"You played brilliantly in that game, Michael," said the Senator. "And I haven't seen you move so fast since that day."

"I don't have too many 300-pound guys chasing me these days, dad. Ugh. It's ancient history. Nobody wants to see that."

"I'd like to see it," said Matt. He would rather have died than watch that doofus shine, but this was all about fitting in, and if the Senator and Caroline wanted to watch the game, he'd watch it, too.

"Well, I wouldn't," said Michael standing up. "I'm going down to Lisa's house."

Michael did play brilliantly. Matt was furious to discover that he was truly impressed. In a moment of rare candor he asked Michael later that evening, "Why did you give it up? I don't get it."

Michael's eyes took on a faraway look. "I felt a calling, Matt. It was impossible for me not to follow where it led. I gave some things up, but what I got was infinitely better."

What an idiot. His girlfriend, the girl in the photo, was gorgeous. And he'd given her up. He'd given up playing college ball, which Matt had to admit he was good at. Who does that? If things like that had fallen into Matt's lap he'd have jumped on the chance. If he had been brought up with this guy's luck he'd have really made something of himself.

The other siblings were ok. They were all older and married. One of Caroline's sisters had a house just down the beach from her parents. She and her husband were kind of cool. Her husband was some sort of financial whiz guy. One of the brothers was a doctor and the other was a lawyer. Both sisters were editors, and the one with the beach house worked from home. The younger sister, Kelly, was also married to a guy who worked in finance. There were a passel of nieces and nephews, so many that Matt couldn't keep them all straight. He didn't care for kids and mostly ignored them.

To be honest, all of the Wallaces treated Matt pretty well to his face. But he knew they must be constantly judging him. And the minute the twin, Michael, stepped into the house all attention, including Caroline's, turned to him. He was polite and friendly to Matt, but his handsome face and tall slim build reminded Matt of all the jerks in high school who had looked down their aristocratic noses at him. He was bound to be arrogant, just like all the quarterbacks Matt had known. Matt had to watch his weight, and it was a pain. It seemed unfair that this guy stayed slim with no effort. Everything had just been handed to Mr. Perfect on a golden platter.

Over time, Matt was there for parties, went to football games with them, and went to church with them. He was introduced to some famous politicians and a couple of celebrities. None of the Wallace kids seemed to try at all to impress anyone, so he adopted a cool demeanor as well. It was maddening. They had no idea what it was like to be a nobody. It was so unfair that they had been handed everything in life. They lived in this amazing beach house and everything came easy to them. Well, Matt was going to have a beach house someday. He was going to have important people drop by to see him. He was going to be somebody. Maybe his future father-in-law would help him get into politics.

The wedding was amazing. Matt asked his cousin to be his best man. He didn't have friends. Most of the guys he knew in high school and college were losers and jerks. Caroline's brothers were his other attendants. The cousin and Matt's parents were the only ones from his side to attend the wedding. His parents wanted to invite some friends and relatives, but Matt put his foot down. He didn't want to be seen with those yokels in front of all the important people that the Senator knew. Caroline's family and friends took up the rest of the huge church. He could see from his parents' eyes that they were impressed. He hoped they wouldn't do anything to embarrass him. He couldn't believe that he'd had the bad luck to be born to those two old fogeys. Well, he may not have been born a Wallace, but he was certainly a member of the family now.

The reception was at a swanky country club. Only the best for Senator Wallace's youngest daughter. Matt watched nervously as his mom and dad chatted with Senator and Mrs. Wallace at their table. They seemed to be getting along fine, but it was obvious to Matt that his parents stuck out like two sore thumbs in this elegant place. Senators and congressmen came over to talk to the young groom, and some of them gave him advice as he'd be taking the bar exam soon. The President of the United States sent a gift. It was the best night of his life.

But late in the evening somebody set up a karaoke machine. Everybody started chanting for that moron, Michael, to sing. The brothers and brothers-in-law beckoned for Matt to come and be a backup singer with them. He'd be damned if he was going to back up the high and mighty Michael at his own wedding. His parents were charmed and sat there fawning over this guy they didn't even know at their only son's wedding. Caroline watched her brother with shining eyes. Mr. Perfect. Then Michael and Caroline sang a duet. They stood with their backs together, with their stupid matching hair almost intertwined, and the photographer went wild snapping pictures of them. Caroline had taken off her veil and was wearing a wreath of white flowers on top of her curls. With Michael in his tuxedo, tall and handsome, and Caroline in her white dress and flower crown they looked like they were in some freaking stage show. Like this day had occurred just for the two of them. Everybody in the crowded banquet room applauded and cheered. Caroline should have been singing with him, her new husband. Never mind the fact that he didn't like to sing. He wasn't interested in karaoke, but that wasn't the point. She was his now. The evening was spoiled.

Matt flunked the bar exam. Caroline passed. He got a job as a teaching assistant at the college and studied to take it again. He flunked again. Caroline was pregnant at this point. She helped him study. She reminded him that John Kennedy Jr. hadn't passed until his third try. Their son Greg was born, and in short order Caroline was pregnant again. Matt wanted a big family, like the Wallaces. He wanted to show off a bunch of well-behaved, beautiful children to their future high-class friends. He flunked the bar a third time.

He would have to teach. Caroline said it didn't matter. She said he'd be a great teacher. She was clerking at a law firm and making pretty good money, but they weren't rich. She didn't seem to care. It was easy for her to do without things. She'd had every advantage growing up. He'd never had anything. They were living in a crappy house just like the one he grew up in. I mean, it seemed like her parents could have bought them a nice house. They were loaded. Caroline never complained, but he knew she must be judging him. He kept up his act. He was a good actor. He knew that someday they were going to live like her family did. They'd have everything money could buy, and people would admire him for it.

Matt drew the line at doing women's work, so Caroline worked during the day and did all the girl stuff in the evening, like cleaning and cooking and laundry and taking care of the kids. Those kids. I mean, he loved them. Sure he did. But they were just always around. There was never a break from them. Caroline wasn't moving up the ladder at work because she insisted on having time to spend with them. It was the one area where she wouldn't budge. She didn't seem to care that she could be making way more money. She actually told him they had everything they needed. This was not the life of high-powered friends and fancy parties that he had envisioned he'd have with her.

By the time they'd had two more kids Matt had completed his schooling and become a History Professor. It was an ok job. He liked standing in front of huge auditoriums and having students listen to what he had to say. It wasn't a very important job, though. He was sure the Senator must be disgusted with the way his perfect daughter had married such a loser. They bought a bigger, nicer house. But it wasn't on the ocean. It wasn't a mansion. Matt knew he was stuck now. The Senator was not going to get him into politics. He had to face facts. He was not even going to be a lawyer, let alone a congressman. He was going to live this dull suburban life with a bunch of loud kids and a wife who didn't put him first. And Michael, that damn Michael, had become a sought-after speaker. Everything that guy touched turned to gold without him lifting a finger for it, and he obviously didn't have a care in the world. He had it easy. He wasn't saddled with a bunch of rowdy kids. When they went back to North Carolina for visits Matt felt like his nose was being rubbed in it. He could tell they were looking down at him. He just could not stand living like this.

When he visited any of the Wallaces he noticed every expensive item in their homes and mentally kept a scoresheet. He obsessed over the huge fancy houses and huge fancy cars and successful children they all had. Well, all except for that weirdo, Michael. But even he was successful in his chosen field. When you thought about it, it was really the Wallaces' fault that Matt hadn't realized his dreams. The Senator hadn't lifted a finger to help him. Caroline wasn't a good helpmate at all. She wasn't one bit interested in increasing their social standing. She spent all of her free time in jeans, gardening and baking and chasing around after the kids. His kids were always dirty and loud and underfoot. Sometimes he'd look out into the backyard and see them all laughing and it seemed to him that Caroline and the kids had their own secret life. Without him. He didn't want to play ball with them or push them on swings or help in the garden. He wasn't interested in those things. But they should have been showing him more deference. Giving him more attention.

And Michael had some kind of weird hold over Caroline. She seemed to put him, and for that matter everyone else, before Matt. It wasn't right. She adored her brother, and he couldn't understand why. The guy didn't have money or a wife or kids or a house or an important job. His dad was a rich Senator, but Michael drove an old Honda Civic. And still, they all idolized him. Everything was Mikey this or Bubba that. His own damn kids were crazy about their uncle, and seemed to prefer him to their father. His own damn parents were taken in. If he heard one more time about how kind Father Michael was because of a letter or book he'd sent them, or how they'd seen one of his talks online and it was so inspirational, he was going to snap. This guy was actually stealing his parents with his sneaky, insincere gestures. He heard them bragging about Michael to their friends. They should be bragging about their son, not some egotistical nutcase who was practically a stranger to them. Caroline and the kids talked to Michael on the phone and FaceTimed with him all the time. It was sickening.

Matt started drinking more heavily. He had to do something to get his family under control. He decided it was time to put his foot down. His parents needed to remember exactly who their son was. It was Caroline's job to make him happy and to help him to be successful in social circles. It was her job to pay attention to him, not her goofy brother. It was his kids' job to make him proud the way the Wallace kids made the Senator proud.

CHAPTER THIRTY-TWO

EVIDENCE

The physical evidence was finally coming to light, but it was tricky. A hurricane of blood had torn through the Carter house. Almost all of the victims had blood splatter from other victims on their clothes and bodies. Sorting out the timeline, and seeing how one person's blood got on another person's clothing, was tedious and time consuming. Blood spatter experts studied Matt's clothing for patterns of his own blood and the blood of the other victims. The biggest question was how young Greg's blood got on Matt's clothing. And then there was Michael's blood. Matt claimed he hadn't seen Michael in the family room that night at all, but there was a spray of Michael's blood on the arms of Matt's shirt and more on his pant legs. Matt's own blood was on top of the spatter indicating that his injuries came after Michael's. They examined Michael's shirt and coat for signs of debris that would match Matt's shoes. They examined the shoes for threads from Michael's coat and clothing. A speck of dirt on Michael's shirt matched the shoes. Two fibers stuck into some blood on the bottom of the shoes were consistent with the wool in Michael's coat. It wasn't much, but they decided to bring Matt in for formal questioning and hope to pressure him into making a mistake while they waited for the evidence to keep increasing.

He was gone.

Matt's parents nervously told the agents that their son told them he needed to get away from all the pressure for the weekend. They had expected him back on Sunday night, but when he didn't arrive they just thought he needed a longer break. They were sure it was just a misunderstanding. He wouldn't leave his son. He wouldn't leave them. They gave the agents the name of the hotel where Matt had a reservation. He'd never shown up to claim it. He was gone.

****

The three of them met in a dirty motel room. Wayne Foster spoke for himself and his brother, Earl.

"We want money. That's all there is to it. You aren't going to get some big fancy inheritance now. But you must have some money. We want it. We need to disappear."

"Now, wait. Think," said Matt. "I can still get the inheritance. The police are sniffing around but they don't have anything. All they have is one eye witness. He had a head injury. I don't even think he remembers anything at this point. And if he can't testify, we're all home free. If he can't testify we just have to sit tight for a bit. I'll get the money, and you'll get a mil apiece. That's worth waiting for. We just have to make sure he can't testify. It is not too late."

"What about your kid?" asked Earl.

"Let me worry about him. He's a baby. He can be made to believe anything. And if he can't? Well, we'll cross that bridge when we come to it. My parents' house is old. It could burn down."

Wayne said, "Why should we trust you at this point? If they pick you up then you're the one who's a risk to us."

"Listen. If Earl hadn't bungled it in the hospital we wouldn't be in this mess. But it's still worth waiting. It's a million dollars for each of you. A million. I'm not a risk. I am going to be sitting pretty with that inheritance someday. Acting is the thing I'm best at. I will act the part of the injured husband. Unfairly accused. I'll give interviews. The media will love it. As far as they know I've never heard of you two guys, and there is no trail to you. I'm no dummy. I've used a burner phone every time. Got them when I was out of town and paid cash every time. I got the initial payment through very convoluted means. They'll never trace it. I'm telling you, even if they do take me in for questioning it's going to be ok. We stay cool and you get a million dollars at the end of it. A million. But you have to stay cool."

"Yeah? Well how are we going to make sure he doesn't testify? They guard him really carefully now."

"I have a plan."

****

Even though no one had a good description of the Wayne and Earl, all three of them changed their appearance. Glasses, beards, different hair colors, and caps might not fool people up close, but they would do for the surveillance. They stayed in different crappy motels, moving every few nights. Matt had a secret stash of money, but it wasn't going to last forever. They needed to get the job done and then get him back home. He'd use the excuse that he'd had a small breakdown because of the constant suspicion and pressure. He'd play the broken-hearted husband and father. He would weep when he heard that Caroline's beloved brother and his favorite brother-in-law had been murdered. He'd rant that he felt this nightmare would never end. He could make it work.

They rented small boats, different ones so as not to cause suspicion, and drove slowly past the Wallace houses at different times of day. Michael was a creature of habit. In good weather he brought his breviary down to the ocean to pray early in the morning. Usually a guard accompanied him but kept his distance. After that Michael would walk or run on the beach. He couldn't go far, but was getting stronger. The guard usually jogged alongside him. Sometimes one of the teenaged nieces or nephews ran with him. In the afternoon he stayed close to the house, swimming, napping or reading by the pool, or staying inside. A couple of times he walked down to the Senator's house, his house now, and spent the afternoon there. A guard always accompanied him and checked the house before letting him enter. In the evening he was back on the beach, and one or more of the siblings or in-laws was usually with him. Sometimes he'd take a second walk or run on the beach.

It had been weeks since any trouble, though, and the guards were getting a little lax. While Michael said his morning prayers, they often sat quite a way away from him, not paying much attention. They'd be reading or doing something on their phones. Sometimes they stayed up by the pool and let him go down to the beach alone. And they had started letting him walk and run on the beach with a family member while they watched from afar. Matt was pretty sure Michael was insisting on more privacy as he recovered. He'd always been so dumb.

On the weekends either Jessica or Beau would run with him. He wasn't much good at running. It was more of a half limp half jog. Matt didn't know why he kept it up when he looked so stupid. He would have been embarrassed to have people see him running in that gimpy way. But Michael kept running and went a little farther each day. Eventually he got to a point that was around a small bend and out of sight of his sister's house for a brief period. Perfect.

The brothers dropped Matt off with a beach chair at the spot they'd chosen. He was going to do it himself this time, and he couldn't wait to put a bullet into that sanctimonious jerk. Three guys on the beach might look threatening, so the Wayne and Earl took the boat out into the water and pretended to fish, waiting to quickly pick him up and whisk him away when it was done. He was wearing a baseball cap pulled over his eyes and had an open book in front of him when he heard their footsteps coming down the beach. He glanced out of the corner of his eye and saw that Michael and Jessica were not paying attention to their surroundings, chatting as they ran. No-one else was with them.

Matt stood up quickly and stepped in front of them. They froze when they saw the gun pointed at Michael's chest.

"Well, look what we have here," Matt said smugly. "Prince Charming and one of the baby princesses. Hello, Mikey."

****

Michael's heart was racing, but he managed to speak calmly. "Jess isn't part of this, Matt, whatever this is. Let her go back to the house." He raised his hands into the air. "I'm not going to resist. Please don't shoot me until she's gone. She's already had too much trauma in her young life. She's just a kid, Matt. Please."

"You want to know what this is, Prince Charming? It's you. All you. You took everything from me; my wife, my kids, even my parents. You've always had everyone eating out of your hand. They couldn't wait to fall all over Mr. Perfect. How does it feel to know that your family died because of you? How does it feel to know it's your fault that your sister died?"

Michael blanched but kept his composure for Jessica's sake. "Matt, whatever I've done has nothing to do with Jessica. I'm begging you to let her go. Do you want me to get down on my knees? Tell me what you want from me."

"I won't leave you, Uncle Mikey," sobbed Jessica. "I won't."

"Please, Jess," said Michael. "If you love me, please do this for me. Otherwise I will not be able to bear it. I'm begging, Matt. I'm begging you to let her go."

"This is all very touching, but I can't do that, Mikey. No witnesses. Well, except for Paul. But he's a baby and nobody will believe him. If they do, I guess we'll have to take care of him as well. Too bad for my folks. They seem to like having him around. They sure never showed me that much attention. She's going to have to die, Mikey, and I think I'll let you watch. Her death is going to be your fault, too, really. You shouldn't have brought her running with you. Think about that for the few minutes left to you. And if you'd just died back at the house like you were supposed to we wouldn't be here, now would we?"

Michael's frantically tried to think of a way to save her. Jess was fast and used to running on sand. Maybe if he could keep Matt occupied for long enough, she could get away. He was pretty sure that he, himself, was going to die on this beach. So be it. It actually felt like some sort of evil circle being completed. It calmed him. He tried to stall while he decided the best course. Maybe the guards would notice they'd been gone for longer than normal and come looking for them. But he didn't want the guards to be hurt either. He remembered Gerry Pelton with a rush of regret.

"Why, Matt? I understand that you hate me. But why the others? Mom and dad were always good to you. They welcomed you from day one. You were part of our family. I don't understand how you could have hated Caro. She was pure good. Did you love her once, Matt? At least for a little while? Did you love those beautiful children?"

"No," Matt answered. "Not even for a minute." He couldn't believe how stupid and privileged this guy was. He didn't even ask about the money.

Michael had occasionally played defense on his high school football team as well as quarterback. He knew how to tackle, but it had been a long time since he'd had a reason to do it. He launched himself at Matt's knees at the same time that he was shouting, "Run, Jess, run!", and in that moment he understood why his sister had said those words to him. His own death seemed insignificant, if only he could save her. He didn't feel the bullet that skated across the top of his ear, or the one that entered his shoulder, but he did feel the impact in his barely healed ribs as he and Matt crashed to the sand. He scrambled and managed to grab Matt's wrist to try and keep the gun pointed away from Jessica, but his hands were still weak from the damage done by the stab wounds.

Jessica realized that the only way to save her beloved uncle was to get help, and fast. Michael could hear her screams as she ran down the beach faster than she'd ever run in her life. The heaviness in his heart lightened as he thought of her getting away. The guards would hear her soon, but it would probably be too late for him. He just had to hold Matt off for a little while longer until he was sure she was safe. Michael fought with all his strength, but felt himself losing ground. He heard a boat pulling close to the shore and felt a bit of hope. He'd noticed two fishermen earlier. Maybe they saw what was happening and could help him. Then he heard some shouting from one of the houses on the beach. Wayne Foster gunned the engine of the small boat as he turned it out to sea and sped away.

****

The McLernan family had a Sunday tradition. Once a month mom, dad, and the two McLernan sons and their families went to early Mass together and then spent the day at Dr. McLernan's ocean front house. As Dr. McLernan and his wife got out of their car they heard terrified screaming coming from the beach. Jeff and Cory McLernan heard it as well as they helped their wives get the children out of their vans. Jeff shouted, "Stay here" to his wife as he, Cory, and his dad raced for the beach. They saw two men struggling as they reached the sand. Jeff, a policeman, noticed the gun right away. Without considering their own safety he and his brother Cory jumped into the fray. The two guys' wrists were twisted together as they struggled for the gun, and since it was impossible to tell which man was the aggressor, Jeff stomped hard on both of them to pin the gun to the sand. Michael and Matt, ironically, shared the pain of a broken wrist. Cory wrenched the gun out and tossed it aside. They noticed a small boat speeding away.

Dr. McLernan hadn't owned his ocean front house for long, and he and the boys didn't know their neighbors. yet. They weren't sure what was going on with these two guys, but dragged them apart and stood over them as their dad called for help. Cory McLernan, an EMT, pulled off Michael's shirt and used it to push against the shoulder wound to apply pressure and stop the bleeding. He looked familiar to Cory, and there were nasty scars all over his chest and arms. Wait. Was this Father Wallace? The guy who'd been attacked with his family when his dad, the Senator, was murdered? Two guys were running down the beach toward them with guns drawn. Jeff, Cory, and Dr. McLernan put up their hands when the guys flashed FBI credentials and told them to sit down on the sand. Within minutes they were surrounded by policemen and FBI agents.

Jessica pushed through the crowd, dropped to her knees, and hugged Michael as she sobbed. Dr. McLernan noticed Michael wince.

"Honey. You're hurting him," he said gently.

She gasped, let go of Michael, and sat back on her heels.

"You're not hurting me," Michael lied. "I'm ok. Just a little sore." And then he added, "You were so brave. Thank you, Jess. You saved me."

"I wasn't," she sobbed. "I didn't. It was these guys who saved you."

Michael smiled at her. "It was you, sweetie. They did save me. But you gave me the strength to keep fighting until help arrived."

****

Frank had driven the shaken siblings to the hospital. "Michael," he said, looking down at the emergency room bed. "We've talked about this."

Michael laughed and then moaned. "I'm trying, Frank. Really I am. And there's not as much blood this time, right?"

"Not as much blood? You look like somebody poured a bucket of it over your head. It seems that you've got nine lives, Bubba, but you've certainly used up several of them. If the McLernans hadn't come along just at the right time, if that boat had been able to land and his buddies could have helped him... well, somebody must be looking out for you. Pretty sure your sister is having a talk with God about now."

"Matt Carter is in custody," Agent Pierson told him. "His partners got away in a boat and we don't have a line on them yet, but believe me a net has been thrown over this whole area. Matt is trying to tell us the gun was yours, that you were carrying it for protection. He says he only wanted to talk to you because he felt you unjustly blamed him for what happened in Portland, and you attacked him for no reason. It's ridiculous, of course. He totally discounts what Jessica saw and says your family has always had it in for him. He still seems to think he can talk his way out of anything."

The agents left him in peace then. His ear, which had been bleeding profusely, was sewn up. He would have surgery to remove the bullet from his shoulder and a cast put on his wrist, but could probably return home in a day or two. His siblings stood around his bed, something that was beginning to feel normal to them.

The mood had turned very somber. Even though they'd known it was Matt who coordinated the Portland attack for a while now, hearing what he'd said while ranting on the beach had made it more heartbreakingly real. This man who had been in their lives, a part of their family for ten years wasn't who they thought he was at all. He was a murderer. He had taken such precious things from them forever. They stood in a depressed silence.

Suddenly Michael started to shake. The adrenaline had worn off and, in his mind he was back on the beach looking at the gun. He could see Jessica's frightened pale face. He could feel the terror, thinking she would die because of him. The gun. He felt a pillow over his face and couldn't breathe. He heard the nurse screaming. He was lying on the family room floor in his sister's house. He saw knives raised in the air. He saw blood dripping down the front of the refrigerator. He could hear Caroline crying. Visions of Maddie and his mom flashed across his mind. The knife. It was so big. He saw his dad's eyes as the life left them. He felt the incredible pain in his chest as his ribs were crushed. He saw Matt's maniacal face looking down at him. Tears welled up in his eyes, and he gasped for air.

"Mikey?" said Lisa in a panic. "What's happening?" "Tommy! Does he have another injury that we can't see? Is he shot in the chest? He can't breathe! Tommy!"

Thomas put his hands on his face. "Michael! What's going on. Where does it hurt?"

But he didn't hear them. He could not stop trembling or control his breathing. He could not stop seeing and hearing and feeling wave upon wave of horror. He blinked and pulled his head away from his brother's hands. His arms flew up in front of his face in a defensive gesture.

"No," he moaned. "Caro. Jess. No." The graph of his pulse rate raced across the monitor where it was being broadcast. All of the graphs started spiking alarmingly.

"I think he's having a panic attack. Flashbacks."

Nurses were already racing into the room. They paged the emergency room doctor, who added a sedative to Michael's IV.

His pulse slowed down, his eyelids begin to droop, and he regained his awareness. He managed to gasp, "Please. Somebody tell me something good. Please. Anything. I can't seem to... I can't... Please. Something good."

Kelly took his hand and stroked it. She spoke quietly. "I'm pregnant, Mikey. I'm going to have a baby girl."

He drifted off to sleep desperately clinging to that thought.

CHAPTER THIRTY-THREE

INHERITANCE

Michael had a plan. First, he discussed it with Dr. Green, and then with his Uncle Bill. Finally, he called his siblings together.

"I have an idea. Something I'd really like to do. But I need to make sure you all agree. I love you all so much and hope you will approve. I want to give away my inheritance. The money, and the house and everything. I don't need it. I'm a priest forever, and have everything I need. It would be a shame for that lovely house sit empty most of the time. It needs a family.

Lisa and David have this house on the beach, and they've told me I have a home with them here. I'm almost ready to go back to my normal life, and they say that my room here will forever be my own. I feel peaceful here. Tommy and Joe, you and your families seem happy living in the city near your offices. You have beautiful homes and friends and neighbors that you love. Your kids are doing well in their schools and love being with their friends. Amy and Sara are very involved with the schools, and everything is nearby and convenient for you and your families.

I'd like Kelly and Stephen to have the house. They both work from home and have small children who can really enjoy the ocean. The house will stay in the family that way. I'm pretty sure Kelly and Stephen will welcome us all as guests."

"Mikey," said Kelly softly. "Are you sure? It's your home. Dad and Mom wanted you to have it. Maybe you should think this over."

"I've thought about it a lot. I'm not going to change my mind. I want you to have the house. Keep what furnishings you want. If there is anything special that anyone else wants, give it to them. Sell the rest. Do whatever you want with it. It's yours."

Tears ran down Kelly's face. "I'll never touch your room, though, Mikey. That will stay the same.

Stephen added, "You'll have two homes. One here with David and Lisa, and one with us."

Thomas spoke up. "I think that's a brilliant idea, Bubba. I am all for it. And for what it's worth you always have a place with Amy and me as well."

Joe said, "I second that. You are welcome at our house any time for as long as you want to stay. We love the beach, but we also love the life we've built in the city. I'd be thrilled to think of Kelly and Stephen making that house their own."

And Lisa added, "I'm tearing up just thinking of a baby bringing new life to that house. And I'll be right down the beach to babysit. It's just the perfect answer."

Then Tommy added, "But the money, Michael. I think you should get some advice before you do anything drastic with that."

"I've already talked to Uncle Bill at length about all of this. He's convinced me to keep a portion of it in an account for emergencies. When I die I can will it to the church. But I want to give most of it away. It's too much and I couldn't be who I want to be if I kept it. I don't think Dad ever realized that. I have some particular charities in mind. And I'd like to give something to the hospitals that took care of me when I was hurt, and also to the individual people, if that can be done.

I don't know how you'll feel about this next thing. I'd like to give some money to Matt's parents. I don't know why he turned out the way he did. I think he's a sociopath, but I can't blame them for it. They're good people. I believe they did their best and now they are suffering greatly knowing what their son has done. I know they loved Caro. They lost a daughter-in-law and three beautiful grandchildren. People will be cruel to them for what Matt did. Maybe they'll have to move. I'd like for them not to suffer financially. Uncle Bill says to wait until after the trial. He wouldn't want any of the money to somehow funnel to Matt. But someday I'd like to try and take care of them.

And another thing. I think we should broach the subject of Paul coming to live with one of you. I wish I could take him, but obviously that's not possible. I know Matt's parents love Paul. But I'm not so sure they are capable of raising him with all they have yet to go through. I wouldn't want it to turn into an ugly fight, but I think we should gently ask them if we can take Paul. He'll be happier in a family with other children. They can see him as often as they want. We can get him whatever counseling he needs, and he'll be protected from some of the horror of people knowing what his father did. It shouldn't have anything to do with the money, though. The money can come later. It's not a bribe or a payoff. I want Paul with us and I want to help the Carters. They are completely separate things. We need to find out about Paul right away."

All four of Michael's siblings and their spouses agreed that they would be willing, and in fact would welcome the chance to raise Paul with their own children.

CHAPTER THIRTY-FOUR

HOME

Michael slipped, without fanfare, into the rectory one Sunday evening. No one seemed to be home. There were so many normal things he hadn't done in months that felt odd to him. His brothers had retrieved his car for him a week ago, but he hadn't driven it until tonight. He hadn't had a fast-food burger until this evening. He hadn't carried luggage or done any physical labor. Even being alone felt strange. His family wanted to help him move, but it was important to him that he do things on his own now. It exhausted him to get his things up to his room and put away, but it felt good to be home. When he opened the door to his room, he noticed that the small bed had been replaced with an extra-long twin sized bed with a thick, comfortable mattress and a new quilt.

Matt was in jail awaiting trial. He was still insisting that he was innocent and being railroaded by a powerful family. He hadn't given the names of his partners, insisting that he didn't know who they were and that they'd committed the murders themselves, possibly because of a grudge against Senator Wallace. But Michael felt safe. Those guys were hired guns. He couldn't really identify them, and they didn't care about him. They were probably as far away as they could get at this point. The person who wanted him dead was behind bars. He couldn't be followed around forever, and his family reluctantly agreed. They dismissed the bodyguards.

His body wasn't totally healed, but the therapists gave him exercises to do at home. He promised his weeping sisters that he would eat healthy meals and get enough rest. It was time to reclaim his life and be back on his own.

Early Monday morning he limped into the kitchen. "Maybe you could teach me to make eggs," he said softly. Eleanor Murphy whirled around and stared. She dropped the bowl she was holding and burst into tears. Michael, embarrassed, apologized for startling her and bent to pick up the broken pieces of china. She pulled herself together.

"Father Michael. Just what in tarnation do you think you're doing?"

Michael stood up and grinned at her as he recognized their old routine. "Gosh, Mrs. Murphy. I thought maybe I could help."

"Have I not told you to stay out of my kitchen?"

"Many times, Mrs. Murphy. Many, many times."

She walked over and hugged him. "Welcome home, Father," she said. "We've missed you."

"So I see my bed has been switched out for a longer one," he said, grabbing a piece of bacon off a tray and munching on it.

"Listen, Father. It's not a sin to sleep comfortably."

"I know. But the old bed was fine. I guess my ridiculous brother just couldn't stand it."

"Actually, Father Clark had the bed replaced. He said he didn't realize how small and uncomfortable it was."

"And why did he suddenly realize that?" He bent over and tried again to clean up the broken bowl, but she waved him off with a dish towel.

"I'm sure I wouldn't know. Now you scoot. Go amuse yourself while I fix breakfast. I do not have time for your foolishness this morning. Go play the piano or something. And I've been talking to your sisters. I'm sorry, but now that I've met them we've become friends. They told me that when you came back I wasn't to listen to any nonsense about you not being hungry. You're to eat healthy meals and take care of yourself."

****

Michael's life became a series of one meeting after another. He had his regular parish meetings and committee meetings. He met with the bishop and had a frank talk about his future. Much to his relief he was going to be assigned fewer speaking engagements. By far the most stressful meetings were the ones with FBI agents, prosecutors, lawyers, and forensics experts who were preparing him for Matt's trial.

It was made clear to him that, since he was the only likely witness, Matt's defense team would work really hard to destroy his credibility even to the point of trying to destroy his character. This was going to be the biggest battle of his life, and he needed to be ready. He didn't tell them that he'd already been through the biggest battle of his life and felt confident about handling just about anything at this point. He was weary, but there didn't seem to be any choice except to keep on going. They took him through what he'd seen and experienced. But they also threw in random questions, specifically designed to catch him off guard and rattle him. They were deeply concerned about his mental and emotional state and the possibility of him being triggered into a flashback while he testified. They felt he was not ready and needed to practice again and again.

"Is it true that you have obsessive/compulsive personality disorder?"

"I don't think so, no."

"But you've seen a therapist about this. Correct?"

"I saw a therapist when I was nine years old for anxiety. My parents were concerned that this might have been the cause of a stomach ulcer. I also saw one after the attack on my family. There's nothing wrong with seeing a therapist."

"Don't volunteer information, Father Michael. Don't give your opinion. Don't be defensive. Always, always just answer the question. Just state facts. So, then. Is it true that you can't bear even the smallest imperfection? That you change clothes obsessively?"

Michael laughed. "Will they really ask that? What does changing clothes have to do with anything?"

The detective sighed. "Father Michael. You need to take this seriously. I don't think you realize how bad this is going to get."

"Ok. I do change my shirt if it gets stained, but not obsessively. Doesn't every... Ok. No. That's all. I do change my shirt if it gets stained, but not obsessively."

But those were the easy questions. They moved on.

"What is your relationship with your niece, Jessica? Is it true that your father had to ask you to wear a shirt around her and her friends?"

Michael stood up with clenched fists. "What? Who told you that?"

"Now see? That reaction is not going to be ok at the trial. You are going to have to be calm and answer some vile questions. Their whole goal is to discredit you, and it will be easier to do if they can upset you. Making you seem emotionally unstable or defensive will help them. Try again. What is your relationship with your niece, Jessica? Is it true that your father had to ask you to wear a shirt around her and her friends?"

Michael sat down. He closed his eyes and swallowed. "Jessica is my niece. We enjoy some of the same things like music and books. I never took off my shirt in front of her or her friends unless we were swimming. There were always other people swimming with us including other men and boys. None of the men or boys in the pool wore shirts when I swam with them. We wore swim trunks, like normal people. It's true that my father once asked me to put on a swim shirt. He said he was worried about my reputation. Because of his job my father worried excessively about what other people thought. Things were always being taken out of context in the news, so he was extremely wary about appearances. My father was wrong. Swimming is normal family vacation behavior for us. My parents and siblings have pools. I grew up living on the beach. Also, I'd like to think I have a close relationship with all my nieces and nephews, not just Jess. I'm their uncle. I love them, as I love all the members of my family."

"You're volunteering extra information again. And opinions. Do not explain yourself. You are not on trial. As painfully frustrating as it may be, just answer the question with facts."

"Those are facts."

"You think so? You do not need to say that you thought your father was wrong to feel the way he did. You do not have to explain that having your shirt off while you swim is normal vacation behavior. The phrase 'like normal people' sounds arrogant and judgmental. They will jump on that. You brought up loving all the members of your family. And here's why you should not volunteer information. Because here's where they will say, 'Ah. Thank you for bringing that up. Is there any truth to the rumor that you and your sister, Caroline, had an... unnatural relationship?'"

The color drained from Michael's face. He stood up and said, "Excuse me for a moment, please." Then he went into the bathroom and vomited. He understood now what they would do. The nightmare wasn't over, and the only way to climb out of this horrible darkness was to live through it. He would do it for her. He hadn't been able to save her life, but he would fight with all his strength to protect her memory. The truth would save them both, and end this madness. It had to.

He rinsed his mouth, went back into the family room, and sat down. He said calmly, "No. My sister and I cared deeply about each other as siblings and friends. There was nothing unnatural about our relationship."

CHAPTER THIRTY-FIVE

MICHAEL

Michael walked, with only the slightest of limps, into the intensive care unit at the Portland hospital and went up to the desk. Jackie looked up at him and asked, "May I help you?"

She didn't recognize him. He was wearing jeans, a black sweater, loafers, and a gray puffy jacket. He carried a backpack over one shoulder. He was clean shaven and his curly hair was well-cut, shiny, and clean. It had been very important to his siblings that he have the scars on his face repaired by a plastic surgeon. Despite his lack of interest, it was easier to just give in, since it meant so much to them. After the surgery he dutifully applied the scar reducing ointment, mostly due to Lisa's nagging. He now had an almost, but not quite invisible line across his right cheek and one on his forehead. They only stood out, white and shiny, when he flushed from embarrassment or anger.

He said, "Jackie?"

She looked up again, studied him for a minute, and gasped. "Father Michael?"

He grinned at her. "Michael Joseph Ignatius Wallace. How's that for being conscious?"

Her eyes filled with tears. "You were so proud of yourself for knowing your name that day."

Michael laughed. "But only until I realized I had no idea where I was. Pride goeth before the fall."

In his backpack Michael was carrying 54 envelopes. Each one contained a hand written, personal thank you note and a check from him for ten thousand dollars. He'd had his uncle Bill check through records to find the names of every single person in the hospital who had taken care of him while he was there. He'd given a hefty donation to the hospital as well, and one to the hospital in Wilmington. For the first time he felt good about the money his parents had left him. Giving it away was going to be very rewarding.

Jackie took him into Dr. Manton's office where he stayed an hour greeting and visiting with some of his caretakers. Dr. Manton commented on the good job the plastic surgeons had done on Michael's face and asked about the scars on his chest and arms. These still looked jagged and cruel, but Michael downplayed their severity. Dr. Manton shook his head. "We honestly never thought you'd make it," he said.

"My one regret," said Michael solemnly, "is that I always thought if this priest thing didn't work out, I'd try and get a job as a bathing suit model." They all laughed. He distributed the envelopes and asked Jackie if she'd deliver the others to the people who weren't working that day.

He and his siblings had arrived last night and were here for the duration of the trial. The others had driven by Caroline's house that morning, wanting to feel some sort of connection. Michael stayed at the hotel. He never wanted to see that house, or even that street again. But he saw them still in his mind. The dark front porch, the long driveway, the dim light at the back of the house, the mud room. Apparently, he had walked very near Gerry Pelton's body on his way into the house, but hadn't noticed him lying there in the dark.

After the hospital he stopped at the Carter house. Mr. and Mrs. Carter were horrified and ashamed at what their son had done. It was hard for them to look Michael in the eye. They were wracked with conflicting emotions. Matt was still their son. They had loved him and cared for him, but whatever they did never seemed to be enough. He'd always been so dissatisfied and negative. But he'd never been violent before. He'd never seemed seriously troubled. They wondered if they should have realized he was mentally ill and gotten him help. It was unthinkable that he was just evil. They wanted to stay home from the trial. But he was their son. And their son was so alone.

Michael gently reassured them. He understood if they did not want to come to the trial. It might be unbearable for them to hear the details of what had happened that night. But if they did, he knew they had to sit near Matt and show him their support. They were his parents. Michael told them that the Wallace family would never think less of them for supporting their son and would forever be grateful for the love they had shown to Caroline and her children. He told them that he was sure that Matt loved them, and had once loved Caroline and the children as well before everything went wrong. It was a generous lie. He would never repeat the words Matt had spoken on the beach when asked about loving Caro and the children.

"No. Not even for a minute." That was a burden Michael would carry alone.

****

Witnesses weren't allowed in the courtroom until after their testimony, so Michael waited in the hall with his siblings and Dr. Green. She had prescribed some anti-anxiety medicine for him, but the first day would be prosecution questions only, so he decided to wait until he really felt he needed it. She also gave him some exercises to do if he started to feel panicky. Focus on a particular spot in the room. Tense up various muscles and relax them. Don't be afraid to ask for a break or some water, but try to do it calmly. Other methods would not be so easy to do if you were paying attention to questions. And Michael needed to think carefully about every word that came out of his mouth. He didn't care what they said about him, but he was not about to let his sister's memory be dishonored.

They called him in early on the third day of the trial. He was surprised at the number of people in the courtroom. Since Matt was accused of murdering a United States senator, cameras and reporters were allowed in the room. Dr. Green told him not to look at Matt. The prosecutor told him not to look at Matt. He looked anyway. Matt stared back at him looking insolent. The Carters sat directly behind him, and there was a tear running down Mrs. Carter's face. Michael resisted the urge to smile encouragingly at her for fear it would be misunderstood.

The prosecutor, Mark McLauren, asked very few background questions. He didn't want to open up avenues for the defense attorneys to dig at Michael. He asked his name and his relationship to all of the deceased. He asked his profession, even though Michael was wearing a black clerical suit. And then he started taking him through the day of the attack. He asked why Michael was in Portland and why his parents came with him. He asked what time he had arrived at the Carter house and what time he left for the church. He had a video of Michael's talk at the Mission and played a portion of it for the jury. It was the very end.

"It's time to forgive yourself." He heard himself say on the video. "It's ok, C."

The camera panned to his family in the front pew. Mom, dad, Caroline, Matt, Greg, and Annie. The two littlest children had remained home with a sitter. Mr. and Mrs. Carter sat next to the Wallaces. When Michael finished speaking people started milling around in the aisle and he watched himself walk down to meet his family. His dad shook his hand. His mom hugged him. Caroline. He could hear her whispering to him and feel her breath on his ear. Michael felt an intense sadness wash over him. That was the last time. The last time.

"I'm sorry. I didn't hear the question."

"Father Wallace? Do you need a break?"

"No. I'm sorry. I just need the question repeated." He struggled to pay attention.

And then he took Michael through the evening in minute detail. The lemon cookies. Asking Frank what could possibly happen to him between the car and the house. The dark porch. The mudroom. The boots. The blood. Maddie.

He felt his heart start to race and the white scars stood out as his face flushed. "Excuse me," he said calmly. "Would it be possible for me to have a glass of water?" While he waited, he chanted, "Little cake-face" to himself.

It went on for hours. It went on forever. He was brought lunch in a small room where he sat alone, per his request. Mark McLauren and his team wanted to discuss how the morning went, but he couldn't face it and insisted he needed a little solitude to regroup. It was harder with his siblings. They wanted, as usual, to gather around and wrap him in their love. He gently explained to them that he needed to think quietly and calm himself. He tried to eat a few bites because Dr. Green had said it was necessary to help with the anxiety. But he spent most of the time praying.

The afternoon was much the same. Mom. Annie. Blood. The sounds. The smells. His dad's eyes. Caroline. The pain.

"Father Wallace? You've stated that someone hit you in the knee, smashing your kneecap and making you fall to the floor in your sister's family room. Who did that?"

"I didn't see who did that. I just suddenly found myself on the floor with a huge amount of pain in my leg."

"It was a compound fracture, correct?"

"I guess. That's what they told me later."

"So you couldn't really move at that point? Because of the pain?"

"I tried to sit up. But I. Well, I just couldn't."

"Your medical records show that you were hit in the face with a pipe, splitting open your cheek and forehead and fracturing your cheekbone and your skull. Did you see who did that?"

"Yes. It was my brother-in-law, Matthew Carter."

"You've stated that a man spoke to two other two men in the room, asking them to hurt you. Who was that man?"

"Matthew Carter."

"Your medical records show that both of your arms were broken with some sort of blunt instrument, presumably when you put them up to defend yourself. Who broke your arms, Father Wallace?"

"That was the other two guys. The ones with the stockings over their heads. I don't know who they are."

"You've stated that a man stomped on your chest numerous times breaking your ribs and collapsing your left lung. Who was that man?"

"Matthew Carter."

"You've stated that a man told the other two men to 'finish her off' speaking about your sister, Caroline. Who was that man?"

"Matthew Carter."

"Father Wallace? You were experiencing lot of pain and trauma that night. Are you sure? Could you be mistaken?"

"I've known Matt for 10 years. I saw him clearly. I know his voice. I know his face. He was standing over me. It was Matt. Matthew Carter. I'm not mistaken."

"Your honor? We don't have any more questions for this witness."

****

Lisa had booked a suite for Michael. He thought it was extravagant, but she knew they would want to gather in his room so she insisted. They sat now on couches in the sitting area talking quietly. Michael was in the bedroom lying on his stomach on the bed with his head buried in his arms. Kelly went in to him.

"We're going to go down to the restaurant to get something to eat," she said tentatively.

He shook his head.

"Mikey," she stopped.

"I'm ok, Kel. I promise. Just sad and tired. It was... a lot. I'd like to be alone for a bit."

"Dr. Green says you should take a sleeping pill."

"We'll see. I don't want to be groggy in the morning. Tomorrow is going to be really important."

"You don't want to be exhausted from being up all night, either, though."

"Ok. We'll see."

"I'll bring you back something to eat later. Ok?"

"Sure."

"Bubba? I'm so very proud of you."

He turned onto his side and looked at her. "We're going to get through this, Kel. We're going to be ok. Maybe not right away. But someday. We're going to do it for them."

****

Phil Gates, the defense attorney, walked to the witness stand. "You dislike Matthew Carter, correct?"

"Yes."

"He wasn't good enough for your sister in your eyes, or in the eyes of your family, isn't that right"

"No. It's not. I was happy for Caroline when she married Matt. We all were."

"You were happy that your sister married a man you disliked?"

"I didn't dislike him at that time. I. I didn't know him then."

"Father Wallace, are you a homosexual?"

"Why would that matter?"

"Just answer the question."

Mark McLauren stood up. "Your honor…"

The judge looked at the defense attorney. "Mr. Gates, is there a reason for this?"

"There is, your honor. And I'll get to it very quickly."

"Please answer the question, Father Wallace," said the judge.

"No."

"No, you won't answer the question, or no you're not a homosexual?" asked Gates snarkily.

"I'm not a homosexual."

"So, you're attracted to women."

"Yes."

"Had any affairs?"

Michael didn't bat an eye. "No. I took a vow of celibacy."

"But you're still attracted to women."

"Yes." He knew what was coming and was ready for it.

"So, you some kind of saint or something?"

"No." That wasn't the question he'd been bracing himself for, and he couldn't keep his face from flushing. The scars on his cheek and forehead once again became prominent.

Mark McLauren stood up. "Your honor, please. This is just badgering."

Gates said smoothly, "I withdraw the last question." Then he said, "So what kind of women are you attracted to?"

McLauren stood again. He started to say, "Really, your honor," but Gates shot out another question.

"Tall slim women with long dark curly hair?"

Michael looked at him calmly. "I'm not attracted to women because they look like my sister, since that's what you're implying."

"Your sister was a beautiful woman."

Michael sat still and looked at him.

"Father Wallace?"

"I haven't heard a question."

"Are you claiming you weren't physically attracted to your sister?"

Michael was grateful that the preparation had readied him for this moment. He looked the attorney straight in the eye without flinching and said, "My sister was a beautiful woman, but I wasn't physically attracted to her. I loved her dearly, as a sibling and a friend."

"You're a handsome man, Father Wallace, or at least you were before you were attacked."

McLauren flew to his feet. "Your honor!"

Gates smiled. "My apologies. Was your sister attracted to you in any unnatural way?"

Michael laughed and said, "No. She wasn't."

"Do you find these proceedings funny?"

"Not at all. I find that question absurd."

"Isn't it true that she called you constantly? In many of the photos we've seen she has her arm around you or is touching you in some way."

Mark McLauren stood up again. "Your honor. I object. This is getting ridiculous. Touching? Of course Michael and Caroline touched each other. They were siblings. Let the defense attorney produce picture of them touching inappropriately. He can't because it doesn't exist. It doesn't exist because it didn't happen. What is the point of this other to besmirch the reputations a dead woman and a crime victim? Could we please move on?"

"Sustained," said the judge. "Let's move on, Mr. Gates."

Michael hadn't taken the sleeping pill or the anti-anxiety medicine that Dr. Green had prescribed. He was tired, but felt strangely calm. It was almost as if he was outside his body watching as the defense attorneys hammered at him incessantly. They accused him of being vain and arrogant. They accused him of being anxious and obsessive. They accused him of being petulantly unable to cope with even the smallest thing that didn't go his way. They suggested that his lack of food, except for the two lemon cookies, on the night of the attack had impacted his blood sugar and made him light headed and confused. They implied that all of the Wallace siblings used whatever means they could, and especially their wealth, to dominate anyone they disliked. They implied that their client had never fit into the tight-knit Wallace clan and made a handy scapegoat.

McLauren objected a few times, but in general let the day unfold. Michael was holding his own, and it seemed better to keep the trial moving.

"Father Wallace, isn't it true that you were questioned several times after the attack on your family, and each time said that you could not identify your attackers?"

"Yes." It was so hard not to elaborate, but Michael sat quietly and waited for the next question.

"And isn't it true that you only identified Mr. Carter after several weeks of being coached by your family and your attorneys?"

"No, it's not. There was never a time when Matt's name was suggested to me or even mentioned by anyone in reference to the men who attacked us."

"You suffered a fractured skull, correct?"

"Yes."

"And when you woke up after a week in a coma you didn't know where you were, or even your name or how old you were?

"I knew my name. At first I didn't remember the other things you mentioned."

"Isn't it true that the trauma, your probable blood sugar spike, and the head injury could be making you remember things incorrectly?"

"I'm not a doctor. It's true that I had trouble remembering things when I first woke up after the attack. As I recovered, memories about that night came back to me. They've all proven to be accurate. I believe that my memories are real. And they are correct. Matt Carter did this to us." Michael paused. He had had enough. He continued, "And it was proven to me when he told me so, just before he shot me on the beach."

The room went wild. The judge banged his gavel repeatedly for order.

He knew. He knew he wasn't allowed to say that. He said it anyway.

"Your honor! I move that Father Wallace's last statement be stricken from the record and he be charged with contempt of this court!"

They didn't charge him with contempt. Michael got a warning from the judge, but in the end they couldn't break him.

CHAPTER THIRTY-SIX

MATT

Everybody tried to talk Matt out of testifying. But he was determined. Those damn Wallaces had kept him in jail long enough, and it was his turn to tell his side of the story. He was a good actor. And he was smart. They'd see. He was going to convince them all and get his inheritance in the end. The money was rightfully his. Twenty million dollars would take him far. Well, eighteen after he paid off Wayne and Earl, but still. Maybe when things settled down he'd sue the Wallace family for more. They'd give it to him, too, if he let them keep Paul. Whatever. He was tired of playing the good dad act. He didn't need some dirty clingy brat hanging around. He'd use the money to really establish himself and get the respect he deserved. Maybe he'd run for office. He could win, too, because people would feel sorry for him. He'd lost his whole family, after all. Everything was going to go his way as soon as he testified. He couldn't wait.

The shooting on the beach was more problematic, but even though that asshole Michael had mentioned it, the prosecution was not allowed to bring it up at this trial. He'd cross that bridge when he came to it. People could see that Michael had it in for him. He was sure he could get through that trial as well. Then it would just be a matter of waiting until he got his money.

It filled him with glee to see Michael squirming in the witness chair, but he kept his composure. He was a good actor. His mom, his own mom, cried when Michael testified. His parents had been under that jerk's spell from the day they'd met him. They liked him better than their own son. Every time Michael stuttered or asked for water it showed what a wimp he was. Matt loved seeing those white scars stand out against Michael's reddened face when they embarrassed him. He loved it when his lawyer implied some kind of unsavory relationship between Michael and Caroline. Those twins were downright weird, and everybody would be able to see it now. Sure, Michael denied it. What else could he do? But the seed of doubt was planted now, and Matt couldn't have been happier about that. Maybe after things quieted down, in a few years or so, Matt could get rid of that guy forever. Send him to be with his precious twin where he belonged.

Phil Gates started taking him through the night of the attack, and he was on fire. He told his story about hearing noise in the kitchen and then running footsteps. He explained about the two guys bursting into the room and how everything happened so fast. He added some facts, saying that he now remembered that those guys had been ranting about Senator Wallace and some of the things he had done. If Michael could remember things long after the attack, so could he. He described the pain of the stab wound to his chest, his broken arm, and the black eye and split lip he'd received. He stressed that his life had been in danger. Michael wasn't the only one who'd had a chest tube inserted. His lung had collapsed, too, and that was incredibly painful. He was the one who had suffered the most. He'd lost his entire family. He even managed a tear for poor dear dead Caroline and his sweet children. He glanced at his mom. She had a look on her face that he could not identify, but she was not crying. She'd cried for Michael. Why wasn't she crying for him, her own son?

Gates asked him about his relationships with the Wallace family members. He said that they'd always treated him badly. They were arrogant and condescending. They knew he came from modest means. Their idea of a husband for Caroline was somebody from a rich family like theirs. Michael, in particular, seemed to really have it in for him. The only reason Matt could see for that was that Michael was jealous because Caroline loved him. Their relationship was weird, and he had thought that living far away from her twin would be good for her. He'd never shown Michael anything but kindness and respect. It was difficult to visit the Wallaces, but for better or worse they were Caroline's family. And he loved Caroline so deeply that he was willing to put up with their unkind behavior. He wasn't surprised that they were trying to railroad him now. It was probably his punishment for marrying their sister and taking her away.

The Wallace family was allowed in the room now, since their testimony was completed. Matt looked at them defiantly. Michael was looking at him. He didn't look angry or upset. It almost looked like he was pitying Matt, which infuriated him. He looked away. He couldn't afford to react.

Then it was the prosecutor's turn. Mark McLauren stood up with a sheaf of papers in his hand. He glanced at Matt. "Professor Carter? You've testified that you always treated your brother-in-law,

Michael, with kindness and respect. Did you have a habit of calling him Prince Charming?"

"That was a joke. Mikey knew I was kidding about that. Jeez. He and Caroline were the prince and princess of the family. I didn't mean anything by that."

"Is it true that after Father Wallace comforted your three-year-old son who was upset over a burned marshmallow that you told him to stop interfering with your family?"

"I don't remember saying anything like that. I might have. Caroline consulted him a lot. I wanted her to break away and devote herself to her husband and kids. He had some kind of weird hold over her. But, even so, he was always welcome at our house. I don't know why he'd think I said that. I guess he just doesn't like me much."

"Professor Carter, you've testified that Father Michael Wallace was not in the family room with you. How do you explain the fact that you had his blood splattered on your clothes?"

Matt blinked. "I don't know. There was blood everywhere. I didn't see Mikey in the room at all. Maybe when I was out of it and those guys were stabbing him his blood sprayed all around."

"How do you explain the fact that your blood was on top of Father Wallace's blood on your shirtsleeves? Wouldn't that mean that your injuries were inflicted after his, that he must have been in the room before you were injured?"

"Listen. The Wallace family is trying to make me the scapegoat here. Their man, Frank Malone, was in that room. Maybe he sprayed some of Michael's blood on me when I was out of it."

"Professor Carter? Mr. Malone didn't arrive at the house until you had already been taken to the hospital."

"Well, somebody else, then. Maybe the guys who did this were setting me up so they wouldn't get caught. I just know that the evidence was tampered with. There was lots of blood."

"Professor Carter, how do you explain the fact that Michael Wallace's blood and threads from his coat were found on the bottom of your black dress shoes?"

"See? This is what I'm saying. The FBI? They worked for Senator Wallace. Lots of powerful people are embarrassed because they can't solve this case. They planted evidence."

"And how do you explain the fact that your son, Paul, said he saw you pushing his uncle with your foot?"

"That's a lie. My son never said that. You're making that up. He's a baby. He was upset and didn't understand what he saw."

"So, which is it? It's a lie? Or Paul doesn't understand what he saw?"

"This is all part of the conspiracy. If Paulie did say that, he was coached."

And that was it. McLauren said that he didn't have any more questions for Matt. But then he turned to the judge. "Your honor. I'd like permission to call some witnesses who weren't available earlier in the trial."

Phil Gates stood up. "This is the first we're hearing of these witnesses, your honor. They weren't included in any discovery."

"Your honor. These are the witness I mentioned in the note I sent you this morning. I think it's important to the state's case for them to be heard."

"I read your note, Mr. McLauren, and feel that there are extenuating circumstances for these witnesses not to be included in the discovery. I'm going to allow it."

"Well, I object," said Phil Gates.

"Overruled," said the judge.

"Exception!"

"Noted. Please proceed, Mr. McLauren."

Mark McLauren said, "The state calls Wayne Foster."

The door opened, and Wayne and Earl Foster shuffled into the room in handcuffs and wearing jail uniforms. It was over.

CHAPTER THIRTY-SEVEN

That Night

There were actually five eyewitnesses to the attack; Michael, Paul, Matt, Wayne, and Earl. Michael and Paul had limited memories because of the trauma and the time they had spent unconscious. Matt, Wayne and Earl knew. They knew of the messiness, the noises, the adrenaline, the panic. They knew. And Wayne and Earl told it all in return for an assurance that they wouldn't get the death penalty.

****

Matt

He played it over in his head as they told it, trying to figure out where he had gone wrong. He'd been so smart and thought he'd considered everything. He was good at planning. The Senator's visit was perfect. It would look like some nut case stalkers had attacked them. At first he offered Wayne and Earl $50,000 apiece. That was a lot of money, and they were in for pretty much anything. But they said that killing babies was over the top. They drew the line there. So the price went up to a million dollars each. They'd have to sit tight until he got the inheritance, of course. They were still reluctant about the kids. Matt told them that they probably would not have to do any of the children, but he couldn't be sure. They just had to be willing, if that's the way things played out. He told them it would be easy. Just quickly dispatch everybody, kind of like in a war. It would be over in no time. Except for Caroline. He wasn't just doing this for the money. He wanted her alive. She had spoiled his whole life plan and deserved punishment. After that, they would wait for Michael. He needed to see what he had done by making himself first in the lives of Matt's family. He needed to die in despair. When it was over Wayne and Earl could rough Matt up a bit. Not too much, but enough to look real. It would be painful, but he had to keep his eyes on the prize. The money would make it all worthwhile. They would call the cops right before doing it, so he would be assured of surviving. Help would already be on the way as Wayne and Earl escaped.

They started with Gerry Pelton. That was easy. While the Senator had been getting death threats and ugly letters, most of them were from crackpots. It was kind of part of the job. They guarded him very carefully in Washington D.C. and in North Carolina. But this was Portland. His visit with his daughter hadn't been widely publicized. It felt safe. So Gerry checked the perimeter every so often, but wasn't on high alert. This was a lovely, upper class neighborhood. Wayne and Earl were waiting by the garage and surprised him. His guard had been down. It didn't take long for the two of them to slice the knife deeply across his throat. He was gone in mere minutes.

At the appointed time Matt went upstairs under the pretext of using the bathroom and killed his oldest son, Greg. The boy never knew what hit him. He was sitting at his desk playing a computer game. He was wearing pajamas and the baseball cap Matt had given him for his birthday. Actually, Caroline had bought the cap. But Matt's name was on the package. Caroline felt that a boy should get a cap from his dad, or some such nonsense. The kid loved that damn cap. Matt hesitated. This was the only one of his kids who was ok. Matt actually enjoyed going to Greg's baseball games and being able to brag about his son. But then he thought about the money. About ridding the world of people he hated. And about the time Greg had drawn a picture of his uncle Michael for school. Matt clapped his hand over the boy's mouth, pulled his head back, and ran the knife across his neck. It didn't go deep enough the first time, and Greg started flailing around. Matt almost panicked. He did it again, this time deeper. Minutes later he lowered the lifeless body of his 7-year-old son quietly to the floor. It was kind of gross, but his adrenaline really kicked in at that point. He hadn't taken any drugs, like Wayne and Earl, because the hospital would probably check him for that. But the adrenaline would get him through. He'd thought of everything.

He had blood on his clothes, but the stairway was dark and he went directly into the kitchen. Caroline and her dad were deep in discussion in the family room and didn't notice. Catherine saw his bloody clothing and looked at him with confusion. The fear hadn't hit her yet. She said, "Matt?" just as Wayne and Earl who were waiting outside the door came bursting in.

Then all hell broke loose.

He grabbed Maddie and slit her throat. It was easier this time because he knew how deep to cut. That should have been the end of it. But he kept remembering how that little brat had followed Michael around begging for stories and horsey rides from the moment he'd arrived that morning. She was wearing the pink unicorn pajamas Michael had given her for Christmas. He was filled with rage. Maybe he wasn't constantly showering her with gifts and reading to her and playing with her, but he was her father. How dare she love somebody else more? He plunged the knife into her chest. It stuck there and he couldn't get it out. So he grabbed the knife Catherine had been using to cut up fruit from the counter.

Catherine gasped, picked up Annie, and began running through the dining room. She didn't scream. She must have been too shocked. Wayne and Earl chased after her. They sliced Catherine's throat and then they'd had to do the same to Anne, because Matt was already on his way into the family room. They weren't happy about it, but they had taken some uppers and there was no turning back now.

"Mom? Matt?" called Caroline from the family room. She'd heard the sound of running feet and some odd noises. She and her dad and Paul were all on their feet. Paul saw him and started crying, the little wimp. None of his kids were worth anything. Selfish little brats. Matt hit him hard with the pipe he was carrying and Paul slammed into the wall and then slumped onto the floor. That turned out to be his first mistake. He should have made sure that brat was dead. Caroline screamed. He turned, grabbed her by that damn curly hair, and yanked hard. He held the knife to her throat. "I wouldn't move if I were you, Senator," he said. "One tiny movement, and she's dead."

The Senator was no fool and no coward. "She's dead anyway, isn't she," he said as he started to charge toward Matt. The old man probably thought he could save her. Pathetic.

That's when Wayne and Earl came into the room and made short work of him. He was fairly easy to take down. Now Caroline. "Hurt her however you want," Matt told them. "But don't kill her. Not yet."

Matt panicked for a minute when he heard a commotion in the kitchen. Had somebody alerted the police? Was Gerry Pelton still alive? He looked up and saw Michael Wallace come to a halt in the doorway. His face was a mask of horror. It couldn't have been more perfect. Matt smiled. "Look at this. Prince Charming came home in time to die."

Caroline screamed, "Run, Mikey, run!" just as Matt hit him in the knee with the pipe. The cracking noise was very satisfactory. Michael screamed and fell to the floor. But then he tried to sit up. Matt hit him hard in the face with the pipe. Michael's cheek and forehead split open and blood spurted out. He fell back. But he was still conscious.

"Stop! Don't hurt her!" he moaned.

Matt went and stood near Caroline, although she was beyond getting up at this point. "Mess him up," he said. "Don't kill him."

Wayne and Earl went to work on Michael with the knives and pipes. He threw his arms in front of his head instinctively. His wool overcoat took some of the punishment, and possibly saved his life. They broke both of his arms with the pipes and the knives made it through the coat to his arms and chest, but not as deeply as they would have gone without it.

"Look at him," Matt crowed to Caroline. "So much for that pretty face. He's not so perfect now, is he? Watch him die, you bitch."

Suddenly Matt felt tired of the whole scenario. Watching them suffer was not as satisfying as he thought it would be. They weren't interacting with him. They weren't noticing his power. They were just moaning in pain. There was really nothing special about them after all. He was done. He walked back to Michael. "Enough," he told the brothers. "Finish her." Wayne and Earl turned back to Caroline with the knives.

Michael began trying to crawl to his sister, He tried to grab Earl by the ankles and pull him away, but his broken arms had no strength and he couldn't make them work.

"Mikey, I love you," gasped Caroline.

Michael had a roaring in his ears and did not hear, but her words infuriated Matt. He began stomping on Michael's chest. In his frenzy he did not see his son wake up and edge out of the room. Not paying attention was his second mistake. Michael started gasping for air. "The perfect twins aren't so perfect now, are they?" yelled Matt as Michael and Caroline slipped together into unconsciousness.

They almost didn't have time to injure him. Luckily, he noticed that Paul was gone, and they heard the sirens when they were still quite far off. That panicked them and they knew they had to hurry now. That was when they made another mistake. They hadn't made sure that Michael was dead. He was drenched in blood and very still and none of them thought to finish him by slicing his throat. They quickly punched Matt in the face a couple of times, broke his left arm with a pipe, and stabbed him once carefully in the chest in the spot he indicated. Then they gathered up all 3 pipes and the knives. They stopped in the kitchen and pulled the knife out of little Maddie's chest. No evidence. They grabbed their boots from the mudroom where they'd left them so that the police wouldn't be able to get shoe prints. Then they disappeared into the dark. Matt got ready to play the biggest role in his life. It wasn't that hard. He was hurting and exhausted. He lay down on the floor, draped one arm lovingly over his dead wife, closed his eyes, and waited.

****

One tiny sentence in their horrifying testimony was a gift to Michael. Her last words to him hadn't been "Run, Mikey." They'd been "I love you."

Three days later, after he was found guilty, they escorted Matt out of the room. He'd been sentenced to life in prison without the possibility of parole. Matt had been right about the Wallace family having some power. They used it to ask that the death penalty not be considered. They wanted Matt locked up for their safety, and they wanted him punished. But they did not want revenge. They did not want to kill Paul Carter's dad. They did not want to kill Marilyn and Floyd Carter's son. More pain would not bring back their beloved family members. As Matt left the courtroom he turned and saw his mother crying. The Wallace siblings stepped across the aisle to comfort her. Cameras flashed as they captured the photo which would be on all the news programs that night - Mrs. Marilyn Carter sobbing on the shoulder of Father Michael Wallace.

CHAPTER THIRTY-EIGHT

BEGINNINGS

Kelly and Stephen settled into their new home on the ocean. They kept Michael's room just as it had always been, and there was still plenty of room for their growing family. With the new baby and their adopted son, Paul, there were seven of them now. Paul was receiving intense therapy and being smothered with love by his aunts, uncles, cousins, and new brothers and sisters. He had a special bond with his uncle Michael and they talked over FaceTime almost every day, even if only for a few minutes. He was in his new brother Max's kindergarten class at school and seemed to be fitting in well. The adoption wasn't final yet, but they had been assured that it would go through soon. Matt had lost his parental rights. Grandma and Grandpa Carter saw that it was for the best, and had reluctantly let Paul come to them, but were frequent visitors. None of the Wallaces blamed them for the evil things their son had done, and they were becoming a part of the family. Kelly and Stephen made sure that Paul was able to visit them and they welcomed his new brothers and sisters into their home as well. The Thornton kids all called them grandma and grandpa and they phoned talked over FaceTime often. The Carters suffered greatly because of the guilt of what their son had done, but the love of these beautiful children was a healing balm to them.

Kelly left her mother's sunporch as it was, and Michael still said Mass for the family there when he was visiting. But she gradually began making other changes to make the home their own. Once the baby was born, they had lots of company. The number of Wallace family footprints in the sand between their home and David and Lisa's grew. They continued to have family picnics on the beach, and Michael joined them when he could get away. He divided his time off between Kelly's and Lisa's houses, and felt at home in both.

Michael, too, had been getting intense therapy. He met with Dr. Green at least once a week, and sometimes more. He'd been on an emotional rollercoaster during his recovery, but after the trial a crushing realization of what he had lost threw him into a deep depression. He knew intellectually that the murders were not his fault, but was overwhelmed with guilt for surviving and for being loved by his family. He was determined to reclaim his life because he knew that's what his parents and sister would want, but he was quieter now and more solitary. There hadn't been any silly karaoke songs since the attack. He hadn't pushed anyone in the pool and, in fact, rarely swam himself. He still played the piano, but avoided his family's favorite songs and mostly stuck to hymns. When he visited he spent a lot of time sitting down on the beach and staring at the ocean, and his family let him have his solitude. They hated seeing him so sad and quiet, but Dr. Green told them to give him time. At least he had gained weight, and his physical injuries were healing. Sometimes Jessica could convince him to play a duet. Sometimes he read to the little ones. On rare occasions he smiled.

Today they stood in the beautiful church surrounded by family and loved ones. The baby was being held by her godmother, her aunt Sara. Uncle David, her godfather, stood beside them. Her young cousin, Georgie, stood on the seat of the first pew to get a better look while his brother, Beau, kept a watchful eye so that he wouldn't fall. Her cousin, Jessica, a budding photographer, discreetly snapped pictures.

Her uncle Michael cupped his scarred hand and dipped it into the baptismal font. He lifted it, trickling water over her forehead and dark curly hair as he said, "I baptize you, Catherine Caroline, in the name of the Father, and of the Son, and of the Holy Spirit."

Little Cee-Cee Thornton looked up at her brother, Paul "Bubba" Thornton, who was being lovingly held in the arms of his grandpa Carter, and smiled.